Joe opened the screened door that separated them and stepped inside. He was very quick and graceful about it. She never would have guessed he could move that fast. He had simply barged on in. He came closer to her.

"Malibu," he said quietly, standing quite close, looking down at her. "Late summer. Five years ago. I was doing a concert and I saw you in the first row and I sent a guy around to ask you to come backstage." His hand reached out and caught her arm as she started for the kitchen. "I think it was a week," he said. "There were a lot of other people around...you said you couldn't stay unless your sister stayed too."

The moment of truth. He put one gentle hand on her right shoulder. If she turned her face just a bit to the right, her cheek would be resting against his hand.

"Please," he said huskily, "take off those stupid glasses."

Dear Reader,

The Promise Romance_{TM} you are about to read is a special kind of romance written with you in mind. It combines the thrill of newfound romance and the inspiration of a shared faith. By combining the two, we offer you an alternative to promiscuity and superficial relationships. Now you can read a romantic novel—with the romance left intact.

Promise Romances_{TM} will introduce you to exciting places and to men and women very much involved in today's fast-paced world, yet searching for romance and love with commitment—for the fulfillment of love's promise. You will enjoy sharing their experiences. Most of all you will be uplifted by a romance that involves much more than physical attraction.

Welcome to the world of Promise Romance_{TM}— a special kind of place with a special kind of love.

Etta Wilson

Etta Wilson, Editor

Morning's Song

Suzanna Roberts

Thomas Nelson Publishers • Nashville • Camden • New York

Published in Nashville, Tennessee, by Thomas Nelson, Inc. and distributed in Canada by Lawson Falle, Ltd., Cambridge, Ontario.

Printed in the United States of America.

Scripture quotations are from THE NEW KING JAMES VERSION of the Bible. Copyright © 1979, 1980, 1982, Thomas Nelson, Inc., Publishers.

ISBN 0-8407-7381-1

Her first name was Morning. Her mother had given birth at dawn, and the name seemed somehow both suitable and romantic. She drove a small car—green, dependable, and conservative—and even though today was a long-anticipated day in her life, still she drove with a certain sense of detachment. Joe Hunter would very likely not even remember her. Besides, there wasn't much chance that she'd even be seeing him.

It was nearing noon as she approached Carmel. Morning had driven down from San Francisco, where she had recently been appointed one of the senior decorators for the exclusive firm of Fairwood and Burham. At twenty-three, she had a very good sense of color and style, and her work had become popular. So when she asked—practically begged—for the particular assignment of decorating Joe Hunter's lavish beach house, she got the job with no real problems.

As she turned right and into the village of Carmel, the scent of eucalyptus came to her. It was early autumn and still warm enough to swim in the ocean, at least most days. Expensive beach houses, Joe's included, were farther down the beach. Suddenly the frightening thought came to her: *What if he's there at the house?*

Once, he had told her he loved her. Would he remember that? Five years before, she and several other young Hunter fans had been unexpectedly asked to visit Joe at his Malibu beach house. Morning had been visiting her cousin in California, and they had gone to a Joe Hunter concert in L.A. During one of his songs he had noticed her sitting in the second row, rapt...

She made the right turn and exited off Highway One. This was Carmel, California, home of the rich, famous and successful. If you could afford to live here, you had made it in this world.

Joe Hunter had done that, most certainly. A country boy from the Mississippi Delta, he had first charmed Memphis. In the same way women adored Elvis, they found Joe's soft-spoken ways, his stunning good looks, his Southern manners, and his wild, sensual music the most exciting combination they had seen and heard since his renowned predecessor. Their worship had made Joe Hunter rich. Now, at thirty, he seemed to have mellowed. His music was still loud and angry a lot of the time, but when he sang a love song, women often wept before they cheered and screamed.

Morning turned left toward the Carmel Highlands where the huge, sprawling homes faced the sea. Joe Hunter's house sat on a rising hill, surrounded by cypress trees. The gardens were neatly kept, but the structure was a kind of hodgepodge—an old mansion with added redwood decks and hot tubs.

Well, she'd done it. She was here, at his house—or one of them. Now she must brace herself to see him once again. The truth was, she had fallen in love with him five years before, and she had never been able to forget the week she spent with him.

The wide front door looked slightly bowed from the salt spray that battered it during windy days. The swimming pool was off to the right, and a long beach-front sloped down to the sea. She used a key which had been furnished by his manager and let herself inside a large bare room. There was very little furniture anywhere except for one downstairs room which contained several musical instruments, including a piano.

The room seemed somehow to be full of Joe.

As the surge of gladness came to her, she chided herself for being foolish. She felt nearly certain that he had forgotten her. After all she had left him quickly, suddenly, without a word. At first, she was certain he had called out to her in the songs he was writing. They were brief, sweet, secret messages for her to get in touch with him, to call him, let him know where she was.

During those days together five years before, he had wanted to touch her and make love to her. The very first night he wanted that. He had seemed somewhat stunned when Morning told him she couldn't do that—it was wrong. After that first night, he didn't ask her again. Instead of being less attracted to her, however, he began to behave like a young man who had somehow, to his great surprise, fallen in love.

The sudden reflection of her face in a shell-framed mirror in the hall brought her from her thoughts. She was a smallish girl, not quite beautiful. There was a small bump on her nose and she tended toward thinness. But she had lovely soft brown eyes and her hair was the same golden-brown as her mother's.

Morning left the patio window in the main room of the house and went to the kitchen. She opened her briefcase and was busily measuring the windows when she saw a Jeep pull into the drive to the house

7

through the huge iron gates that she had left standing wide open.

She watched as the driver parked and sat staring at her car which was parked just ahead. Then he got out of the Jeep and walked quickly toward the house. He was tall, wide-shouldered, dark-haired, still gorgeous and still slightly, charmingly sloppy-looking.

Joe.

Her whole being seemed to change. It was as if some invisible, scented, warm breeze touched her, filled her with hope and something close to joy. Seeing him on videos, on television, and on record album covers was not the same as now, watching him gracefully leap up the steps to the front veranda. She lost sight of him as he crossed the porch to the side door. She was certain it was locked. There was a moment of quiet when he must have been searching for keys. Then, seconds later, the front door was tried and opened.

"Okay," he yelled from the hallway. His voice was loud and confident. "Who's in my house?"

With tape measure in hand, Morning stood frozen to the spot. She could think of nothing at all to say. Besides, she needed more time to gather herself. She had known she would be seeing and talking to Joe Hunter, but she'd never guessed it would be this soon.

"Hey," he called again. "Where are you? Just come on out nice and easy, so I don't have to blow your head off."

"In here," she called immediately. "I'm in the kitchen!"

She fumbled quickly in her purse for her sunglasses. They slipped down on her nose a bit and she hastily pushed them up again. She could hear the sound of his boots crossing the uncarpeted flooring of the hall. She stood, back to the long sink, waiting.

And then he stood in the doorway, filling it. He gazed at her somberly and suddenly began to smile.

"Hi," he said easily. He was deeply tanned. His eyes were still that astonishing blue. He looked the same. No, not the same. Better.

"Hi." She very nearly swallowed. "You're Mr. Hunter."

He was looking at her more intently, blue eyes narrowing.

"Joe. Ah—are you here to interview me by any chance?"

"No," she said quickly. "No. I'm not."

"You're from the *Chronicle*," he said suddenly. "Somebody called about a profile—"

"No," she said, "I'm not—"

He was still watching her. "You've written a song," he said. "Right? You look like a girl who would write songs."

"Sorry. I'm here to decorate your house." But her face was flushed and warm and her voice very nearly trembled. She was glad she'd thought of the big, dark sunglasses. "From the firm of Fairwood and Burham in San Francisco."

"Beg pardon?"

"They—we're decorators." *Why am I putting myself through this? Like a groupie seeking an autograph, like a dog begging at the back door. Here I am, well on into what should be full womanhood, feeling as if I'm eighteen again—*

"Oh," he said, "sure, I remember now. Was I supposed to be here at some certain time?"

"We didn't expect you at all, I'm afraid."

"Well," he said, and he seemed vaguely puzzled, "I'm sorry I yelled at you. And the part about blowing somebody's head off, that was just a big fake. I don't keep a gun around."

"That's very sensible," she said carefully. He seemed to be trying to remember something. She turned back to the window, her back to him. "I'll get on with this, if you don't mind."

"Oh no," he said from behind her, still in the doorway. "You go right ahead. I'll just—listen, would you like a cup of coffee or anything?"

"No, thank you." She wrote down the measurement, her face still burning with emotion.

There was a small silence. Morning moved to the next window, opened her tape measure once again and began. She wished she had not come here. With all her heart she wished that. When the sound of Joe Hunter's voice shattered the wish, she closed her eyes and braced herself.

"Do I know you?" he asked. "Listen...did we...I get the feeling that I've seen—"

"Excuse me," she said quickly, "I want to measure the windows upstairs before I leave."

She knew he was watching as she left the room. At the doorway, he gazed briefly down at her, his eyes puzzled. But he stepped aside politely to let her pass.

She walked across the wide hallway to the curved stairs and began to climb. She did not look back, but she felt sure he was still watching her. She turned around suddenly as she reached the top stair, and half-way faced him. He was indeed watching her.

"I'm sorry," he said from below. "I guess I'm still trying to decide where I've seen you." He smiled that white, crooked, charming smile that had charmed millions of fans. He had a certain teasing naughtiness about him, like an exasperating child grown into manhood, that women adored.

"A lot of women in San Francisco dress the way I do," she told him. She smiled somewhat stiffly and went on up the last stair.

"Wait...somewhere—"

"We might have seen each other at one of those press parties," Morning told him. "I have friends who are journalists." That was true, not a lie in the real sense. She did have a friend who worked for the *Chronicle* and he had taken her to a few elegant press parties. But she had never been to one given for Joe Hunter. She never would have had the courage to go.

"We didn't get introduced," he told her. "I'm—"

"I know who you are."

He was waiting for her to introduce herself. He didn't know her last name. He never had. That had been the problem in finding her. That, she knew, was why he had sent those secret, loving messages in his songs.

"I'm Miss Edford," she said briefly. "From the firm of—"

"Yeah. You told me that." Still watching her. "Well, I'll be down here, Miss Edford, in case you can't get the doors open. It's so damp here sometimes they stick."

"Yes. I'll call down if I need you." She continued on down the wide, breezy hallway toward the master bedroom. Joe had obviously slept here. A few of his clothes were scattered about, but the room was reasonably neat. He must have been well-trained by someone—perhaps his mother or a girlfriend. The spread was even thrown over the covers on the water bed, somewhat sloppily tossed, but done, all the same.

She could hear him moving around downstairs. Opening a cupboard in the kitchen, rattling a pan. Was he cooking? If he cooked and asked her to stay, surely

11

that would mean he knew who she was—and possibly even why she had come here.

She went on about her work. It was foolish to go on hiding her name from him. The truth was, she had come here to see him, perhaps to stir his memory—or was it to ease her mind by finding out he wasn't at all the way she remembered him?

"Excuse me," Joe said from the doorway.

Morning was at that moment on a ladder, second step from the very top. When she gasped and quickly looked over her shoulder, he practically lunged forward from the doorway to catch her if she fell.

"You gave me a terrible start," she said from her perch on the ladder. "You can move away now. I'm not going to fall."

But he stayed put. "What's your first name, Miss Edford?"

She went carefully down the ladder steps, her back to him. She needed more time. He was supposed to be in Los Angeles at a recording session. Hadn't his road manager or his business manager or somebody told Renée that?

She began to gather up her things: the tape measure, the notebook, the color charts. "If you want a bank reference," she said, stuffing things into her briefcase, "my firm has already sent the necessary—"

"I'm not talking about a bank reference," he said steadily, coming closer to her. "What I'm talking about is you." He let his breath out. "Tell me your first name. Please."

"I don't see the need of that," she said primly, stuffing the tumbled wad of fabric samples into the briefcase. Her voice was very slightly trembling.

He seemed to be blocking the doorway. But she wasn't at all afraid he wouldn't move for her to pass.

There was, she remembered, a side of him that was sweetly gentle, always polite.

"I'd like to leave, please," Morning said, banking on his good nature. "If you don't mind—"

Instantly, he stepped back into the hall. When she was halfway down the stairs she heard him call out to her: "I'll think of it. Listen—I'm sorry if I—"

From the foyer she said, "It's perfectly all right," not turning around. She pushed open the swollen door and hurried across the wide veranda and down to her car.

Morning sat across from her boss, Renée, in the dining room of San Francisco's Fairmont Hotel. An exquisite fruit salad for two was in the center of the table. Rose petals were scattered among the pears, grapes and pomegranates.

"It's very important to remember," Renée said as she popped yet another grape into her red open mouth, "if you do a bang-up job on the Hunter house and it sells quickly for a good price, word will get around, dearest, and you'll be in demand. Other people— maybe Hunter's friends—will want you to do their houses, too." She smiled. "You can increase our fees at that point. And of course your own, darling."

"Renée, I'm not sure I want to do Joe Hunter's house."

"You have to be joking, dearest. You are, aren't you?"

"No." Morning looked beyond the carefully made-up face of her employer and gazed across the room. *My father would have liked this hotel*, she thought. He had enjoyed surveying such elegant settings and making glorious fun of all the snobs who, like Renée, sat eating expensive food while they talked ever so earnestly about money. There were times when Morning somehow felt she must turn and run from this woman she worked for. And yet the money was very good, a substantial salary, enough for her to be able to rent the expensive small house on Telegraph Hill, plus send a check to her mother each month to help defray the heavy expense of the private nursing home for her father.

"Look," Renée was saying, "Morning, are you listening?"

"What? I'm sorry," Morning said quickly. "I guess I'm a little tired. I didn't sleep well last night."

"Over there," Renée hissed, "in the doorway. I think that's what's-his-name, the television actor. Smile, darling. Try to get him to stop by the table."

"You smile at him," Morning said suddenly. "Excuse me, Renée, I'm going home."

I could be fired, she thought in the taxi. She gazed out the window. No. She wouldn't be fired. Renée wouldn't fire anyone who was making a lot of money for her.

It was a nice day. Why hadn't she walked partway home, then taken a bus? She was always jumping in and out of cabs whenever she had business in the city. Her mother would call that wasteful.

"Stop here, please," she said suddenly.

"But lady, I thought you said—"

"I want to walk awhile," she told him.

The driver was grey-haired and balding. "Sure." As she paid him, he said offhandedly, "When I've got troubles, I talk it over with God."

She felt shock go through her. "Thanks for reminding me."

That happened to her a lot. God was always putting other Christians in front of her. They seemed to pop into her life with amazing regularity, as if to hold her on the right path. It was almost as if He wouldn't let go of her.

I'm fine, she thought as she walked along the city streets. *I'm still a Christian. I wouldn't do that to my mother, to my father—the way he used to be.*

But somehow, those didn't seem like the right reasons. And the nagging feeling that her life was wrong and getting more so seemed to haunt her. She stood waiting for a traffic light to change, and suddenly she thought, *I want to see Joe again. I feel I need to be near him again. I must still love him! Dear Lord, don't let that be wrong!*

Chapter Two

Morning hadn't been to the office for five days. Presumably she was working at home on a creative plan for Joe's beach house. She had promised Renée she would hand in the specs on it very soon. She needed to stop thinking about Joe's other beach house, the one in Malibu, and the days they'd been together there. This was a different time and place. They were both older now.

She lived in the section of San Francisco known as Telegraph Hill, where the small and humble houses cost a fortune to buy. Her little cottage—or rather the one she rented at a very high rate—sat beside a flower-stew of lilacs and roses and herbs. Gardening was Morning's way of getting close to God, or at least it had been once. She had found her home high above the city and kept herself to the quietness of growing beautiful things. But now, the tiny garden was noticeably neglected.

She made a tuna fish sandwich and stood with it looking at the rain out the kitchen window. She wasn't hungry at all. She wrapped the sandwich, put it in the fridge and decided to settle for just tea. The tea tasted weak and bitter. She'd forgotten to buy honey. What was wrong with her, anyway? She had work to do, a mountain of work to do and she'd better get to it. She must try, try to see Joe's Carmel house in her mind's eye. Imagine the side decks gone, so that the original concept would at least be partially restored. Those ugly hot tubs had to go. Definitely.

You're jealous. Jealous of whoever gets in that tub with him!

She decided to have another cup of tea, honey or not. She started to reach for the kettle when suddenly she noticed a man, a tall man, bounding up the wooden steps of the Hill. She made a small sound, a kind of horrified gasp.

Joe was hurrying up those steps, looking like he was heading straight for her house just off Napier Lane. His dark head was bent in the chilly wind and his wide shoulders were hunched against the thin rain.

Quickly, Morning rubbed the foggy window glass to try to make sure. Panic began to rise in her. She had not, under any circumstances, expected him to show up here. Never. What was he doing here, anyway? She thought for a blind second that perhaps it was some sort of wild coincidence, that he had not come to track her down at all but was looking for another house, some other address. A lot of people loosely connected with "show business" lived on Telegraph Hill.

The kitchen was beside the tiny living room in the front of the cottage. She ran to the screened-in porch in the back to get a better look. No doubt about it. It was Joe Hunter, all right. He strode swiftly and surely up the wooden steps leading to Napier Lane.

Then he stopped, looking no doubt at the number on her front porch. *Renée told him*, Morning thought. *It had to have been Renée who told him where I live.*

He was knocking on her door. Firmly, but politely. She was trapped. She looked around wildly for her sunglasses. If he asked she would tell him they were prescription lenses. She stuck them on and went to the front door.

"Hello, Mr. Hunter. Are you lost?"

He smiled down at her. He seemed very pleased with himself.

"Well," he said cheerfully, "aren't you going to ask me in? I think I broke my leg on that last step."

She didn't smile, although her face had begun to warm.

"I'm very busy just now," she told him. "I've got some ideas about your beach house but I'm afraid I need a little more time to work out the costs." His eyes seemed very bright to her, and he was still smiling a little, as if he knew some marvelous secret.

He opened the screened door that separated them and stepped inside. He was very quick and graceful about it. She never would have guessed he could or would move that fast. He had simply barged right on in.

He came closer to her. "Malibu," he said quietly, standing quite close, looking down at her. "Late summer. Five years ago. I was doing a concert and I saw you in the second row and I sent a guy around to ask you to come backstage." His hand reached out and caught her arm as she started for the kitchen. "I think it was a week," he said. "There were a lot of other people around. You said you couldn't stay unless your sister stayed, too."

The moment of truth. He put one gentle hand on her right shoulder. If she turned her face just a bit to the right, her cheek would be resting against his hand.

"Please," he said huskily, "take off those stupid glasses."

Morning kept her head down. "It wasn't my sister," she said faintly.

"What?"

"I said it wasn't my sister. It was my cousin."

Now, he put his hand against her cheek. Then the other hand on her other cheek. It was, she knew, the glasses he was after. He wanted to see her eyes, look into them.

"Your first name is Morning, isn't it?"

So he hadn't forgotten either.

"That's it, isn't it?" he asked again. "That's your first name."

She had the odd, unexpected feeling that something had begun. It frightened her, but it was exciting, too. Wasn't this what she had longed for, dreamed about for so long?

She closed her eyes as he took off the glasses. He removed them gently, almost tenderly, putting them in his pocket. Now his hands were on her face.

Morning opened her eyes and looked up at him. Just looked, gazed into his summer-sky eyes, but that was all she had to do. She saw, in that brief fraction of time, a sudden look of amazement come into his eyes, followed quickly by what could only have been real joy. And seeing his relief, his gladness, she smiled in return. *Old friends*, she told herself, *meeting again, reunited. Perhaps that's all it is*.

"I knew it," he said softly. "I knew if I could only see your eyes again."

"It's...a striking coincidence, isn't it?" Morning said, and she drew away, her face very warm now, her heart beating hard. "Our—running into each other. After all this time, I mean."

There was a sudden silence between them. He had shown obvious emotion at finding her, but she had kept her feelings hidden.

"I always knew I'd find you again," he said finally.

"Yes," she said, "well…people do run into one another—especially in California." She sounded very nervous indeed. "Would you like a cup of coffee or something?"

"We have to talk," he said, and he was following her through the small dark hallway to the kitchen. "I've been trying to find you for five years, and if you—will you please turn around and look at me for a moment?" His voice got louder. "Why'd you do that? Why'd you take off that way? Listen…I…it makes me so—"

"My father got sick," she said. She took a small breath. "I got a phone call from my mother and she told me. It was—he had a stroke. He's never recovered."

"Oh," he said. "Oh. So that was why." He ran a quick hand over his face and went over to the window, standing with his back to her. In that moment, at the long window, in the lavender-silver light, he reminded her of himself one evening in Malibu, when he had stood this way, legs apart, big shoulders drawn a bit forward, hands jammed into his pockets. Trying to reason through whatever the conflict was. The first time, five years ago, it had to do with her decision not to allow him to make love to her—

"No last name," he said quietly. "I was so hung up on you, on your first name, on the songs and words that kept coming into my head during that week that I never got around to asking you what your last name was!" He shook his head and turned around to look at her. "Can you believe that?"

"I'm sorry," she said quietly. "I should have—gotten in touch with you."

"You heard my songs? Didn't you hear the messages?"

"Yes. Look," she said hastily, "I'm...I'm sorry! I suppose I thought it didn't—that you'd—"

"Forget?" He smiled at her. He had put away the stark emotion she had seen unmasked in his eyes. Now he was once again his cool, collected, charming self. "I'm a very romantic guy. Also a very hungry one. Let's go out for dinner. Wait—first—you're not—I know you aren't married," he said, "because if you were, you'd wear a ring. And you're not—" For a second, his eyes looked frightened. "It's been a long time," he said finally. "Maybe you are married."

"No."

"I knew you weren't," he said, having gathered his charm about him again, teasing her, probably knowing very well that the vast majority of women found him irresistible. "I can always tell if a girl is married. Well, most of the time I can tell. Aren't you going to ask me the same question?"

"I know you aren't."

"Oh? So you've kept in touch, more or less. Checked to see how my life was going since you walked out of it."

There it was again, that quiet anger that somehow managed to show through his good nature and charm, from time to time. Until this moment, she had never guessed that he might be suffering—remembering as much as she was.

Morning went over to the stove and surprisingly began to make coffee. In this moment of strain when conflicting feelings were rushing through her like small tidal waves, she was doing exactly the same thing

22

her mother always did in times of crisis: she was making coffee.

"The call from my mother put me in a panic," she told him. She was busy with the cups and saucers, getting out the best spoons. "I simply bolted and ran, went first to my cousin's parents—"

"She left, too," Joe told her, "the same morning, before I even got a chance to come downstairs."

"I flew home. They took me to the airport. My aunt went with me. I think I was hysterical on the plane. I don't really remember." Unexpected tears came to her eyes. "I thought Daddy was invincible. That nothing could touch him." She went back to measuring coffee. "I suppose the worst of it is that he didn't die. He's still alive. If you can call it that."

"I'm sorry. You should have let me help you."

She shook her head. "No. My mother and I had to get through it by ourselves." She put saucers, cups, and spoons on the table. Their conversation was easier now, kinder, more tender.

"And did you get through it okay?"

"I suppose we did. Anyhow, we're both functioning. Mother's seeing someone. Another man. She felt it was time, I guess."

"Look," he said kindly, "could we go somewhere? I'd like to take you someplace where we could have dinner together. Will you?" He caught hold of her wrist as she started back to the stove. "Please."

"I should be working on the plans for your house."

"Forget that. You've just been given an official time extension by the owner. No hurry, in fact. The later the better." He stood up, making her suddenly feel quite small. "I know a great place. Have you ever had bear stew?"

"Certainly not," she said. She felt wonderful. Her

head felt as if she'd had some kind of magic wine. "I wouldn't dream of eating bears!"

"Good. In that case, Tommy's Joynt is out. I know a great place in Berkeley. The people who run it all think they came here from another planet. Strictly vegetarian. If we hurry we can get there for the pea-pod special."

"Let's stay here," she said suddenly. "I—don't have much food on hand, I'm afraid, but I could fix—let's see—eggs, and—"

"You stay here," he told her. "I'll be back with—do you know how to fry fish? I mean, really fry fish?"

"No," she said. "I don't think so."

"Okay. You make the salad. I'll take care of everything else." At the door, he turned to look at her somberly. "Don't leave," he said. "Don't take off."

She smiled. "I won't."

"Promise? Never again?"

She hesitated for just a fraction of a second, as if some small, clamoring warning was sounding within her.

"Promise."

And she meant that. For the moment, at least.

True to his word, Joe returned, breathless from running up the steps carrying two large grocery sacks, with all manner of good things to eat. Had she ever in her entire life, in her *absolute entire* life, eaten a real Southern hushpuppy, he asked. No, she had not. They were delicious, or at least something she ate was—perhaps she had been too happy, too high on being in the same room with him to really notice.

Joe had a recording session mid-town, so he left soon after helping with the dishes.

He had not kissed her. She knew he had wanted to,

desperately wanted to. But the sudden intensity of their feeling had somehow made them careful, almost shy around one another.

When he'd gone, she stood in the darkened living room, leaning against the chilled window with her plants making their shadows on the painted walls. The house seemed…different, somehow. As if it weren't the same at all. She suddenly knew she would never get the same pleasure from this little place. Whatever steps she had taken to rule out falling in love, they were gone now, disappeared. Now, she wanted to be in love and to know he loved her still.

She didn't sleep very well. She kept waking up, listening. What was she listening for? His step out on the porch, perhaps? Or perhaps another phone call, bringing horrible news, taking her away from Joe once again?

She rose at five. In the little mirror in her bedroom, she peered tiredly at her face. Her wide, dark eyes looked back.

Does Joe think I'm pretty? She honestly didn't know. Besides, his feeling for her seemed to have nothing at all to do with prettiness. If it did, there must be thousands—hundreds of thousands—of pretty girls here and in Europe who would gladly change places with her.

She dressed and puttered about the kitchen, feeling their time together in the room the night before. She waited until what would have been eight-thirty back home and then called her mother. In all their conversations for five years now they had both pretended, very cleverly, to be clinging to the belief that Morning's father was certain to recover. For a time, they had even pretended they believed he would one day go back to his post at the University. They no longer did that,

25

however. They no longer spoke of "When your father returns to teaching." Now they settled for pretending that he was slowly but steadily getting better, when they knew he was not.

"I'm glad you called, dear," her mother said, sounding very close and clear over the miles. "I'm going to a tea at your dad's English department and I have to put on my faculty wife disguise."

Morning smiled, seeing home in her mind's eye, the yellow kitchen and the window in the living room with the violets in white pots on the window seat.

"Are you making coffee, Mother?"

"As a matter of fact," her mother said, "I am. Why?"

"Then you must have something to tell me. I had a feeling," Morning said. "That's one reason I called."

"And what's the other?"

"Mother, I've got something to tell you, too." She closed her eyes. "I think I've fallen in love with someone."

"Wonderful, darling!"

"I don't think I know quite what to do about it though," Morning said. "About him."

"I wish you'd waited," her mother said.

"Waited! Mother, I'm nearly twenty-four!"

"Until after Philip and I—we're talking of—getting married."

Morning had known her mother was seeing a man, of course. Philip was a widower. She had met him in the most approved place, at church.

Morning's throat seemed to have gone dry. "How can you do that? With Daddy—when he's still—"

"We don't know if we can or not," her mother said. "We've only just started to talk about it."

"I see. Well," Morning said, "I'm sure you'll both do what you think best." *For yourselves. Not for Daddy.*

At once, Morning regretted thinking that way. It wasn't fair, that was all. For her mother to…leave him this way. How could she want to be someone else's wife, while he, her father, sat in a chair by a window, but not *the* chair and not *the* window, in that place, and waited? Did he remember any of their life before? Or was he totally and absolutely wiped out forever? Or at least for the rest of his life here?

Morning couldn't tell her mother about Joe and her love for him. Not now.

They hung up with that heavy feeling of separation still between them. Morning decided she would not think about it, not now. She pulled out her drawings and tried to see the house in Carmel in her mind's eye—as it was now and as she would have it. But somehow, another house seemed to get in the way— the beach house in Malibu, five years ago. It had a wide, long deck, and one night he had stood beside her, his arm around her, and asked her to think about marrying him.

What would have happened if…

If.

She took out swatches of material from her briefcase and held them up to the morning light. She wondered if all his places, his houses and an apartment someone said he owned, if they all had that don't-care look about them inside. Hardly any furniture, no curtains, just a bedroom and one other room where his band probably practiced. Lonely men lived that way, didn't they?

And if that were true, how did she know that? How was it that she sensed things about him, knew with a certain heart that he was lonely, that he was looking, searching. For something or someone.

27

His call came at noon. Morning was sitting at her worktable in the kitchen, facing the porch that offered a sweeping view of the city. She realized she was waiting for him to call her.

"It's me," he told her. "I'm at the airport."

"Oh." Her heart squeezed tight. He was leaving, going someplace.

"Did I wake you? Most of my friends go into a coma until two-thirty."

"No," she told him, "I'm fine. I've been up since—"

"Morning," he said suddenly, "I'm on my way to Nashville and I want you to come with me. Will you? There's still time if you hurry."

"I—Joe, I can't do that!"

"It took me most of the night," he said, "to talk myself into asking you to go. And then this morning I lost my nerve again. I don't—I don't want you to think I'm asking you to—"

She was silent.

"At least," he said finally, "not unless you want that too."

Morning gazed out the window at the foggy city. "Joe," she said, "I'm sorry. I think I'd better not."

"Too soon? Am I rushing you?"

"Something like that." She needed time to think it all through. If they were lovers, what then? What if he had changed? What if he no longer thought marriage was a likely outcome of being together?

"You'll be where you're supposed to be when I get back, then?"

"Where am I supposed to be, Joe?"

"Where it isn't very far," he said, "from me. Okay?"

"Goodby," she said.

"Wait. Remember you promised not to run away."

"I won't. I'll be…somewhere not too far from you."

"You just turned on my light," he told her.

Having hung up and put the choice behind her, Morning admitted to herself that she would have liked very much to go with him. To be there in Nashville with him. Yes, to make love with him.

Renée's office was extremely chic, a posh place of plants and mirrors and piped-in music and muted colors. All the lightbulbs were tinted ever so slightly, so that pink was the look of all the glass desks and tables and even some of the chairs.

Now, Morning's boss gazed at her from behind her black-rimmed spectacles.

"I suppose you're wondering why I phoned and asked you to drop by," Renée said, offering coffee from a silver pot. "To tell you the truth, dearest, I tried to call you last night but your phone was off the hook, it seems. I take it you were busy with company or something."

"Something like that, yes."

"Anyhow," Renée went on smoothly, "this meeting is due to a call I had from Joe Hunter's manager."

"Oh?"

Renée smiled. Her smile was radiant. She had spent a lot of money on caps. "Mr. Hunter wants you to move to Carmel while you're doing his beach house."

"He *what*?" Surely, Joe didn't think she'd—

"All is proper, darling," Renée said. "I've reserved a room at a very nice, private hotel in Carmel. You can drive from there to his house in less than ten minutes."

Why didn't he mention that on the phone to me this morning? she asked herself. But once again, she pushed worry from her mind. *Why not go to Carmel, be closer to him?*

29

"I suppose it doesn't matter where I do the work," Morning said.

"We've got a lot of accounts riding on the success of what you do with Joe Hunter's house," Renée said, her eyes narrowed. "I never thought of you as a raving beauty. But you seem to have caught the interest of—what'd they call him today in the *Chronicle*?—the most gorgeous country-rock singer of the decade."

"He isn't just that," Morning said quietly, almost to herself. "Joe can write the most beautiful, haunting music…"

She decided to stop right there and avoid the subject of Joe's music entirely. There were indeed songs he'd written and sung that were filled with warmth and love and a kind of sweet, human longing. She'd heard them during those two years after their Malibu encounter. There were songs about love not lost but missing, songs that begged the beloved to return. There were songs about searching, looking "in all the wrong places" for a dream-girl, someone lovely, known only very briefly, gone like the morning mist. Oh, he had used her name in many of the things he'd written. His work at that time had been an outcry, a secret message to her, begging her to listen, to get in touch—

"Can you be ready to move into the hotel in Carmel right away?" Renée asked.

"You mean today? Surely you don't mean today."

"Today, dearest girl. And do yourself and my firm a great favor, will you? Try to keep on the good side of Joe Hunter. I understand he can be very difficult at times."

It seemed better at the moment not to reply to that. She would go to Carmel, then, just as Joe wanted her to.

30

She had made up her mind to be as happy with Joe as she could be, for whatever brief time they might have together.

By six that evening, Morning was unpacking in the oversized hotel room complete with a small wood-burning fireplace. The hotel was posh and very expensive; Renée thought it looked better for the firm if decorators stayed in the best places while they worked on somebody's house.

She suddenly glanced at her open suitcase and saw her Bible. Her parents had given it to her when she was a child. She knew she could open the first page to find her mother's handwriting, urging her to read daily. Right now, though, she really must get to work.

There had been a small package waiting for her at the front desk when she arrived at the hotel. Now unpacked, with diagrams, figures, fabric samples spread out before her on the writing desk by the window, she carefully unwrapped the small brown package, thinking it might be the rust satin swatch she'd ordered. But it wasn't. It was a tape from Joe. And written across the top of the little box was: "Morning's Song."

About thirty minutes later he called. She could hear sounds in the background, somebody playing scales on a horn of some kind.

"Take a run out to the beach house and play the tape," he told her. "You did get it, didn't you?"

"Yes. I got it."

"Wish you were here with me," he said.

There was a small silence. She wanted to tell him he might have asked her about coming to Carmel, not have someone who worked for him contact Renée and give an order, but she didn't.

"Is something wrong?" he asked.

"No. It's just that—I've got to get back to work."

"Are you mad at me?"

She took a small breath. "Joe," she said finally, "if you want to know…I'm not used to having people tell me where to live while I'm working for them. Even Renée didn't order me to live in San Francisco!"

"So that's it," he said. "Look, all I did was mention to my road manager that I'd be glad if you were in Carmel. I guess he jumped the gun or something. I'm sorry."

"It doesn't matter."

"Will you play the tape? At the house, I mean?"

"Yes. I'll go tomorrow."

"Good," he said. "I'll be back sometime tomorrow." He sounded worried, as if their relationship had already hit rough waters.

"Goodby," Morning said.

He had told her he'd be back tomorrow. Tonight, he'd be standing in front of an audience, and they would yell and scream and clap and cheer. Some of the girls and women would weep. Perhaps they would be waiting for him outside, the way she and her cousin had done the night they'd gone to the beach house in Malibu.

But most of those girls would be willing to make love with him. She hadn't. Would he—

She closed her eyes. *No. I know he won't. He won't do that. Right now, he wants only me.*

And the wonder of that filled her, so that her hand shook as she tried to recapture the train of thought— costs for fabrics, paint, repairs for his Carmel house.

Right now, he wants only me!

The Carmel shops were closed by nine, except for one just down the street on Ocean Avenue that sold ice

32

cream. Morning pulled on her cable-knit rag sweater and walked to the very end of the quiet street where the beach began. She stood watching the dark sea for a while and then decided to walk to Joe's house. She felt much better.

The house was dark and gloomy-looking. She turned on as many lights inside as she could, and realized that she wasn't afraid here, not at all. Joe lived here. It was his house—or one of them, to be more exact.

There was a big note in the kitchen, penned by the person who worked for him, cleaned the house and kept the refrigerator well-stocked. Yes, someone had seen to it that there was food, expensive food, in there for her. The note said for Miss Edford to please help herself. Obviously she was to spend her time here, in his house, not at the Carmel hotel. That meant he wanted her with him under his roof, when he got back from Nashville.

In the rehearsal room on his desk, there were roses, some three dozen of them in three different vases. They scented the room, this room where his books and his piano and gold records seemed to fill the space with his presence. The cards on the roses were all different. One said "Please," another said "don't break," and the final card said "your promise."

And on the desk was a note for her. *"The roses gave me an idea for a song. Title's in the little cards with the flowers. Tape recorder is in top drawer. Joe."*

She found the cassette recorder and took it from the drawer. And suddenly, almost as if a voice whispered to her, she thought: *Aren't you a Christian anymore?*

And boldly, she silently answered: *I love Joe. I need him. I'm sick of being alone and miserable!*

She put on the tape, allowed herself the luxury of

33

sinking back into the softness of Joe's wonderfully comfortable leather chair, there behind his wide desk, and closed her eyes as the music began.

The piece started with a very faint guitar sound, a soft, almost tentative strumming on the lower keys. It grew into a melody after just the right sequence, and then the pure charm of the basic melody began. Joe's voice, quiet, sensual, so intimate that Morning's face warmed, sang to her.

The words spoke tenderly of the world of a young woman he once knew, a woman very vulnerable, filled with joy and love for everyone, but who, when the love of a man comes to her, runs away and hides.

When the song ended, Morning was crying. Tears seemed to pour out of her, long-hidden tears for some lost, happy self who believed in goodness, just as the song said, but who also lived in a kind of child's world, with the innocent view of a child. And out of those tears she shed came the resolve to be happy once again.

Even if what she did was wrong.

She walked back to Carmel with the tape inside her sweater pocket. Morning felt pleased with herself, with the way her life was going. Joe would be back to-morrow.

Chapter Three

The next morning she was awakened by a quiet knocking outside her door. There she found a silver tray with an elegant breakfast on it. She hadn't, of course, ordered it. Another phone call from one of Joe's "people," no doubt. Seeing that she was well looked after, orders from the Boss.

But she enjoyed the breakfast, and with the newspapers under her arm, she walked down to the public beach, found a bench, and opened one of the papers to the entertainment section.

Someone in San Francisco had gone to Nashville to see Joe's show and had obviously called in his review. There were words like "stunning," "a return from rock to love ballads" and "a man in love singing about love—"

Nashville applauded him, boasted of him, loved him as only a brilliant, talented Native Son can be loved. Hunter is not only what every Southern woman wants but what possibly every woman in the world wants her man to be like—

Morning went back out to his house around noon.

From here she could make phone calls to the fabric designer in San Francisco, collect of course, and really begin to pull her ideas together. The sooner she finished her work here, the sooner the house could be sold.

And then what? Now, she had an excuse to be around him—her job. When she was finished here, he would want her for something else. She tried not to think about that as she diligently worked away at sketches and made the phone calls to San Francisco. She even tried calling Renée, to get approval, but her boss wasn't in.

"I can't believe it," he said from the phone booth in Monterey late that afternoon. "You're still there!"

"Of course I am," she said. "I promised, didn't I?"

"Don't go," he said quickly. "Don't take off. I'll be right there. Oh—honey?"

This breathtaking intimacy—he called her that—how had that come about? It was as if she had already promised him she would stay on after this job was finished and over with.

"Joe, I'm really trying very hard to do my job here," she said. "I'm...not sure we...that we should—"

"I'm still rushing you," he told her. "Look, I promise I'll behave, okay? I just want to rest up. It was crazy there last night."

"I read about it. They adored you."

"Yeah. Look, I'll be right there. Any food left?"

"Joe, I wasn't *that* hungry!" She smiled.

"I've got sort of an open-door policy," he told her. "People sometimes wander in and help themselves."

"Nobody came," she said.

"Morning, did you play the tape?"

"Yes."

36

He had said he loved her in the song, but they let that subject drop. "Good. See you in a little while then. Don't go."

She went back to her work, but actually, she knew she was waiting for the sound of a car in the driveway. And it pleased her to have him come back from Nashville and find her here, in his house, waiting for his return.

He had taken a taxi. From the moment he entered she realized there was no need to worry about how he might behave this time. They talked about his concert, her plans for the house, the things he liked to do there.

As the chill that followed sunset entered the house, he built a marvelous fire for her in the living room, using wood stored on the main deck. It was still scented with the sea odors, weed and salt and brine. They blended into a lovely aroma, and as she sat on the floor watching the flames, Morning felt a growing sense of having moved from the "real" world—the world outside this house—into a kind of delicious mixture of another time in another seaside house with him.

Now Joe sat beside her, close but not touching. He was a much quieter man now. The complete self-assurance and sharp worldly outlook had mellowed. He now seemed able to enjoy just sitting here, talking. He didn't try to pressure her.

"Know what I'd like to do, Morning?"

She smiled into the flames. "Something to keep me from getting my work done, probably."

"I was talking about my boat," he said, pretending to be offended. "One of these fine days I'm going to move onto that boat. Nobody can find me there. Nobody can make me go on the road or do a concert or go on stage. Paradise!"

"Then you don't get any real pleasure from your work, Joe?"

He turned his head to look at her. His beautiful eyes were very blue and serious. "All I know right now is...I need you. If I didn't have to worry so much and so often about your taking off, maybe I could think about other things. Like my work."

She knew she should be flattered, happy, to hear him say that. And yet, that small warning voice was there again, telling her to watch out. This was a man who was very used to being adored by women—used to having his own way. Used to using his power to get him whatever he desired.

"In the time since we were together," he asked quietly, "wasn't there somebody in your life? Okay, you never got married, but there must have been some guy who was—somebody you cared for."

"There wasn't," she said, not looking at him, "anyone."

"Okay," he said, and there was pleasure in his voice. He lay back, hands behind his head. "I used to think you'd show up," he said softly. "I went along on that for about a year, telling myself she'll show up back-stage one night, buddy, so just hang in there and be patient. When you didn't, I went through a crazy time. Wrote crazy stuff. Wild stuff. I was mad at everybody. My mother died that winter. My kid brother was acting like he was trying to kill himself and I couldn't seem to straighten him out. When I lost him too—I really went over the edge." He had his eyes closed. "Got into some real rough-sounding music. Electronic stuff. It was very bad."

"But your fans love it, Joe."

"Must be something wrong with them," he said.

"Are you hungry? Say but the word and I'll go put on the steaks."

"Joe," she persisted, "hasn't it…don't you ever think about…about having an obligation to those young people?"

"Sure. I have an obligation to see to it that they get their money's worth."

"I meant—"

He was clearly not willing to discuss that aspect of his work.

"Time for me to do the cooking again," he told her. "Prepare to be dazzled."

And so Morning knew this was something she must not speak of again—responsibility to his fans, to the millions of young people who looked upon him as a kind of god.

There was something so wrong, so terribly and totally wrong with that. It terrified her.

After the dinner, which was just as he'd promised, "splendid," they sat again by the fire, listening to some of his tapes. When she heard the ones he had cut, she knew it was because he wanted her to hear a special song he'd written, trying to find her. Some were tapes of other singers he liked.

And somewhere along the line, she drifted off…

When she woke, he was kissing her. She opened her eyes and very nearly pushed him away. But—

It was so wonderful, so delicious, so—*perfect*—to be here with him before the fire, having him bend over her tenderly, kissing her—

"Maybe I should have waited," he murmured, lips softly against hers. "Maybe it isn't fair, kissing somebody who isn't even awake."

She very nearly smiled. "Joe…you're—"

The need in his eyes was very clear. "Maybe I'd better invite you to go for a swim," he told her. Some look of worry must have come into her face, because he quickly pulled her to her feet and kissed her forehead very softly. "You'll find some bathing suits upstairs. I wasn't talking about skinny-dipping." He grinned. "Although that's not a bad idea either..."

Morning found three new suits, each in a different size, presumably for guests. Her size was one piece, in a modest navy blue and had, he'd told her, been chosen by his housekeeper, a local woman who had very firm ideas about proper behavior.

He turned on the deck lights, which partially lit the beach, too. Joe stood at the deck railing, waiting for her. Without his shirt, wearing only faded jeans, he was muscular, beautiful, a superb young man.

He did not stare at her but took her hand and led her down the deck steps, across the sea-washed sand to the water's edge.

"Good time to swim," he told her. "The water's still fairly warm."

He had taken off the jeans, and as Morning waited he glanced at her, but only for a second. She was glad she pleased him, for whatever reason.

"Can you swim? Never mind; I'll stay close to you."

"Yes," she told him. "I can swim." The water, however, felt somewhat chilled to her. She went in and gasped, coming up.

Joe was watching her, keeping guard over her.

"If I drown," he called, "be sure to give me mouth to mouth!" But he was only teasing again. She saw at once that he was a strong swimmer, as he cut through the waves and began to swim. Her midwestern upbringing had caused her to feel somewhat uneasy in water that wasn't confined to a swimming pool, so she swam fairly near the shoreline, conscious that Joe, who'd gone far out, was nonetheless keeping a watchful eye on her.

Finally, they came out of the water together, holding hands.

"Best time to swim," he told her, "is night. Very late at night. Next time we'll do it that way." He tossed her a big beach towel. "Will you move in here, Morning?"

"What?"

"I want you to move in here," he said steadily, "with me. What's the point of your being in that hotel in the village when you could just as well—"

She wrapped the towel around her shoulders and moved on toward the house. He had looked at her, of course, as she'd gone closer to him in the knee-deep surf. And she was glad she was slender and nicely shaped and that her legs were pretty. None of those things should be really important, but all the same, she was very glad that she was pretty—for him.

"Aren't you at least going to talk about it, Morning?"

"Not now," she said. "Right now I think I'd like to make a big pot of coffee!"

"Okay," he said. "Sorry if I did it again, honey." He took her hand.

"Did—what again?" she asked.

"Scared you," he said, and suddenly, he scooped her up and, despite her protests, carried her up the steps to the deck and on inside the house. He put her down in the living room, where the fire still burned in the huge fireplace.

"Okay," he told her. "Go make the coffee and I'll make all those phone calls about the road tour. Might as well get that over with."

So, wearing a beachrobe she'd found upstairs, her hair wet and curling about her face, Morning went into

41

the kitchen and began to make coffee. She heard Joe go upstairs. After a while, she found a big tray. She put the coffee pot, some cups, and sugar and milk on it, along with some lovely iced donuts she'd discovered in a box on the dripboard. Joe's "people" thought of everything!

Joe was dressed in his usual old jeans, wearing some kind of faded tee shirt that advertised one of his road shows. Morning put down the tray and poured coffee.

"I'd like to kiss you," he told her.

And she heard her own voice, willing and warm, "I'd like that too."

He rose and came toward her, drawing her into his arms. Her eyes were open as he bent his head to tenderly cover her mouth with his own. Then she closed her eyes, put her arms around him, and gave herself to the warmth, the wonder, of that moment—

Someone was knocking at the front door. Pounding on it.

Morning opened her eyes and moved quickly out of Joe's embrace.

"Joe—"

"It's okay," he told her. "I'll get rid of them—"

Morning went over to the fire, putting her suddenly cold hands out to warm them. She heard voices—his and a woman's. Then, her heart seemed to miss a beat. It was Renée!

And in that moment, Renée swept into the room, bringing the heavy scent of her expensive perfume with her. She took a long, calculated look at Morning and then turned back to speak with Joe again. Something about a possible buyer for this house, once it was finished.

But Morning had seen the quick look of reprimand in her boss's face. The bare feet, the tumbled hair, plus

42

the cozy fire and the breakfast tray—

"I'm going to have to take our genius-child away from you for a little while," Renée was saying. "A sort of business meeting in Carmel. Morning, darling, do go and get dressed!"

Her face burning with embarrassment, Morning hurried up the stairs to the room where she had left her clothes.

When Morning followed her boss out of Joe's house, she felt somehow as if she'd been caught doing something she shouldn't. The taxi was waiting; as they pulled out of the driveway, she turned to look back at the house. Joe had closed the front door. She could see the orange reflection of the flames in the great fireplace against the glass of the window.

Renée, beside her in the cab, was silent and distant. The ride from the beach to the hotel in Carmel took only moments. Renée paid the driver and again she gave Morning a cold glance.

"I'm not planning to stay the night," Renée told her. "However, I'd like a word with you in private."

"We can go to the room here if you like," Morning told her, feeling dreadfully uneasy. "Would you please tell me what this is all about, Renée?"

"All in good time, dearest."

In the room, Renée stood firmly in the middle of the room, glaring at Morning. Her eyes were dark and hard behind her glasses.

"You're sleeping with him, aren't you?"

"What?"

"Joe Hunter. You're having an affair with him." Renée seemed to be watching Morning for a reaction. "I thought I made it very clear that I don't allow my people to sleep with clients."

Morning felt her face color in something close to a

guilty reaction. "No, I'm not," she said finally, beginning to unpack the briefcase. "I'm not sleeping with him."

"Then why were you there so late? What were you doing there at his house?"

"I'm decorating it!" Morning's voice was edged with anger. It was an emotion she had little use for, and yet, around Renée, she often felt that way. "That's what I'm supposed to do, isn't it? Isn't that what you pay me for?"

Surprisingly, Renée smiled. "Good," she said calmly. "I believe you. I know you well enough, darling, to know you'd simply tell me to mind my own business if the two of you had decided to become lovers."

"Please," Morning said, "don't ever—ever do again what you did tonight, Renée. Barge in and—and order me out of my client's house as if I were some sort of school child!"

"Agreed. But surely," Renée said, "you can see that sort of...game...isn't good for business. I've been through this before, believe me. One of my decorators slept with Miles Langdon last year, doing his Beverly Hills house, and when they had their first big fight he decided to hire another firm to do the decorating. I just want to be sure—"

"You can be sure that what I've told you is true," Morning said calmly. She had, somewhere during Renée's story about the woman who'd had an affair with one of her clients, decided to keep quiet about her real feelings for Joe.

"Besides," Renée said, still smiling, "I could fire you, you know."

"Then why don't you?" Morning realized with a mild start that it didn't matter. The job, the wonderful, glorious dream job she'd lucked into didn't seem important, all of a sudden.

"Because I like you, darling. I like your talent. I like the way you can pull an old ugly house together and make it lovely. You know how to cut costs and still give it that look of class."

"Thank you, Renée," Morning said coolly. "Are you finished telling me off? Because if you are, I'd like to get back to work on Joe's house."

"One more item, Morning." The dark eyes were steady and cold. "I'd rather you didn't call Mr. Hunter by his first name. It's unprofessional."

"Certainly." Morning very nearly smiled.

"We understand each other then," Renée said smoothly. "To be quite frank about it, I was surprised that you became so—friendly—so quickly. I mean, I always thought of you as a very reserved girl. Downright religious."

"Really? Why thank you, Renée."

'I'll talk to you later, darling. I'd like to see you in my office sometime day after tomorrow."

"You mean you want me back in San Francisco day after tomorrow?"

"And bring your notes and everything else on the Hunter house." Renée picked up her handbag. "See you then. Oh, enjoy this nice room. It's costing the firm a fortune."

With Renée gone, Morning decided to go to bed. She was far too embarrassed to call Joe and explain what had happened. And, she suspected, he was far too considerate to start phoning her tonight, especially when he thought Renée might be there still.

When she got up the next morning, she didn't give Joe time to catch her. She put on her jogging clothes and had just closed the room door behind her when the phone began to ring. She took the elevator down and quickly left the hotel, heading for the beach. There, she began running. The beach wasn't crowded. Only a few young people were out, most of them running as she was. Far down the beach on her left some people were cooking over a fire, having a beach breakfast.

She gave herself to the sheer joy of running, inhaling the smells of the sea, fresh, rain-washed. Her body felt its young power as she went on, and although her mind did not totally clear itself of the unsettled feelings inside, she did begin to feel better.

When she became tired, she stopped and rested on the beach, gazing out at the blue Pacific beyond. And finally, she made herself face the frightening questions: *Why are you going back to Joe Hunter? Do you still belong to Christ?*

It was quiet here, on this part of the beach. She had spent an hour running, running away from facing the possibility that what the world offered seemed so much more worthwhile than what her faith promised, if only she could endure—

She returned to her room and showered and dressed. She gathered up her spec sheets and went to sit on a bench in the pretty little park smack in the center of the village of Carmel. It was late afternoon when Morning finally walked back toward Joe's beach house. If he had tried to call her again, she hadn't been in the hotel room long enough to catch the phone.

She owed him an explanation. At least, she owed him that.

She walked toward the back deck, with its uniform wooden steps leading up to the house. But once in front of the glass door, she suddenly felt like an intruder. She knocked, trying to think of what she would say. She certainly ought to apologize for Renée's behavior, for one thing.

Nobody answered her knock. She thought she heard music coming from somewhere deep inside the house. It had to be Joe, playing a tape. She tried the door and it opened easily at her touch. She walked through the room with the fireplace, calling Joe's name, but there was no answer. The music was definitely coming from his rehearsal room and it was turned up very loud. No wonder he couldn't hear her.

In front of the door, she knocked once, then again. Suddenly it opened and there was Joe standing in front of her, looking totally surprised.

"I've been going crazy, trying to figure out if you were still in town. I finally called the desk at your hotel and they told me you hadn't checked out." He drew her inside the music-filled room, then pulled her close. "What a time for whatever her name was to show up!"

Very gently, Morning eased herself out of his embrace.

"I only came to...to apologize," she said. "For what happened. For Renée's barging in that way."

"It's okay," he said lightly, watching her as if he were trying to figure out what was bothering her. "I deal with crazy people all the time. Dealing with crazy people is a big part of my daily life."

"Just so you understand," she said rather limply.

He went over and turned off the cassette recorder. In the sudden silence, she saw the questioning in his blue eyes.

"Did I do something wrong?" he asked.

She felt he had somehow found her out. "Joe, I'm not at all sure you'll be able to understand this."

"Probably not," he told her, still keeping things

light, joking with her. "I'm not much good on an empty stomach. So why don't I send out for a big Italian pizza? There's this place in Monterey—"

"Joe, I'm not staying."

He frowned. "Oh? Well." And for a second, he was quite serious. "You mean you aren't going to stay with me tonight. Or any other night. Right?"

"I'm sorry," she told him, her voice on the verge of shaking. He could look so boyish and sad that her heart ached to go to him and cradle his head on her breast and soothe him. The very thought of his embrace made her feel slightly light-headed. "I've decided—not to decide at all," she said, "at least, not right now."

His face was serious. Something close to anger flashed in his eyes. "So you walked all the way back here to tell me that you're sorry if you break my heart, but no dice. It's the same thing as it was five years ago. You don't want us to behave that way, right?"

"You're making it sound—"

"Unimportant? Well," he said, his voice louder than it should have been, "maybe that's because right now I'm feeling that whether or not I make love to you isn't the big issue with us anymore! It's something else." He was silent for a few heartbeats, watching her. "There's someone else, isn't there? There's another—"

"Joe, let me explain—it isn't—"

He turned away from her. "I asked you before," he said quietly. "You could have told me then."

Morning realized she had meant to come here and tell him about her beliefs. She had meant to explain to him that, even though her body yearned, even ached for him, there was something inside her head that moderated that desire. She had even thought that perhaps they could sit before that lovely fire and talk about what was missing in their relationship. What—no, *who*—they needed to sustain them, to draw them close, so that their hearts and minds would be merged with His, and the problems that seemed so impossible to solve would be gone like shadows before sunlight.

No, that wasn't going to happen. She knew that, sensed it. She and Joe wouldn't sit together this night and speak of Christ.

"Let me take you to dinner," he said. "We don't have to talk about whether or not you ought to crawl into my sinful sack and stay the night. We don't even have to talk at all. I'll take you to a very nice place on Cannery Row in Monterey, and we'll just sit and silently enjoy all the good food. Then I'll take you for a nice, silent ride on my boat."

She shook her head. "Not tonight, Joe."

"I told you I won't ask any more questions about men in your life, past or present," he said, and his eyes were masked. Whatever emotion he felt because he believed there was another man in her life, he managed to hide very well. "I should have known you weren't telling me the truth when I asked you if there had—been anyone."

The tears came, hot, behind her eyes. He thought there was someone else. Well, let him think that. Because in a sense there was. There was Someone in her life who would not let her go. Someone she belonged to, above all else.

"I'm afraid I'm rather tired." She pushed a strand of hair back from her face. "I'm not dressed to go out. I think I'd like to go back to the hotel and go over some of the notes I made about your house."

"Okay. Listen, I'll give you a ride. At least let me drive you to your hotel."

"If you're sure—" She really was tired now.

Funny—all that running had not tired her at all, but a very few moments with Joe, knowing his hurt, and feeling her own, exhausted her.

He put one arm around her waist as they walked through the empty silent house and down the wooden steps to his Jeep.

He said nothing at all to her on the brief drive to Carmel. In front of the hotel, he leaned over, opened the door on her side, and briefly looked into her eyes.

"See you," he said.

Morning hurried into the hotel. She did not cry until she reached her room.

Chapter Four

This time, he didn't call her. Morning thought of phoning Joe before she left the hotel to drive back to San Francisco, but decided against it. As she pulled her small car into the traffic, she consoled herself with the thought that it was all important to deftly separate their relationship from her job, her assignment to do his house. Business and—

But it wasn't. It wasn't pleasure in any sense of the word. It was not the dream she had dreamed before. Of how, when they saw one another again after so many years, they would somehow instantly go back to the same feelings that had been cut off when she left his Malibu house and fled home to her mother and her stricken father.

That hadn't happened. Joe wanted very much for her to be his lover. She wanted that too. But there was always that warning inside her—and now, driving toward San Francisco, she allowed herself to think some of the worrisome thoughts that she'd pushed deep down into her subconscious before.

Joe had millions of women wanting him. He might have been upset because he now believed that she had a man in her life. But of course, Joe himself had never so much as hinted to her that his own life had been clear of affairs during the past five years! There had been girls, yes. Beautiful girls. She'd read about them in newspapers, magazines, seen him on television at awards dinners with a gorgeous girl on his arm.

She wanted time, time to think things through. Time to decide how to talk to him about her faith. But now that she had that time, and plenty of it, it seemed, she was filled with the yearning to be near him.

She had not counted on this great, overpowering need she felt for him. The way his face would suddenly flash into her mind, like an unexpected photograph on a silent screen, and she'd once again see his smile, the nice curve of his cheek, his beautiful, thick-lashed eyes—

All right, Lord; I did it. I put him out of my life, for the moment, at least. But do I have to feel so miserable?

Arriving in the city, she had breakfast at a drugstore, then walked over to Renée's office. She had, as Renée had instructed, brought along her briefcase, filled with notes and bits of material and colors. It seemed odd that at this stage of the decorating Renée would want a conference about the house. Usually, she let her decorators do as they pleased. At the final moment, of course, Renée checked the figures and costs—that was all.

The girls in the clerical section looked at Morning as she walked through the outer office. Some of them appeared plainly envious. Working for Joe Hunter really was a dream assignment.

Down the hallway, closer to Renée's office, she felt a kind of tightening in her chest. Renée did that to people. Her footsteps were silent on the thick peach carpeting. Renée's office was at the very end of the hall.

The door was closed, as always. Morning's own tiny office was on her left. There were three more just like it—dens of the aspiring young decorators who worked for Renée.

She tapped at the door, then opened it without waiting for an invitation. Renée was on the telephone, sitting there looking very chic, dark hair perfectly styled, make-up giving her a kind of artificially glazed look. She gave Morning a long, chilly stare as she went on with her phone conversation:

"We can most certainly do it in country French if that's what you want, Marcella. I'll send down my expert in that pretty country look—dried flowers and copper and yet elegant. Is that what you mean?" Renée suddenly rolled her eyes at the ceiling. She always seemed to seduce customers, trick them. She never seemed to be able to deal with them openly and with honesty. Only the week before, she'd told Morning that she was sick of people who wanted French provincial.

"It happens to be my favorite kind of look," she went on. "I absolutely adore all that—prettiness." She motioned for Morning to sit across from her. "You'll adore the person I'm sending down to you. Yes—I'll have her get in touch as soon as she gets to L.A. And thank you *so* much!"

She hung up and leaned back in her leather chair.

"That was that old hag, Marcella Stratton. She wants us to do her house for her. She's getting married again. I think this makes five or six times. It doesn't matter."

"Do you mind if I ask why you wanted me to come in, Renée? I've got a hundred people to call about fabrics for Joe Hunter's house. I've got appointments—"

"That's why I called you in, darling," Renée said smoothly, "I'm taking you off the Hunter assignment.

53

You'll have a very big job working out plans for Marcella Stratton's honeymoon cottage. I believe it has some twenty-eight rooms in all."

"You—you're going to take me off the—Carmel job and—" Morning's voice faltered. *At least I wouldn't have to see him. I wouldn't be tempted to get into an affair and get hurt—*

"You aren't going to have a tantrum or anything, are you dearest? That would be so unlike you." Renée smiled, pushing a folder toward Morning. "Here are the ideas she's mentioned. The old girl wants it very cozy, lots of flowers and—"

"And who'll finish up on Joe Hunter's house in Carmel?"

The smile broadened. "I will, darling. I'll give it my own personal touch. I'm sure he'll understand, if I tell him you aren't feeling well or something." Her eyes went cold. "Unless, of course, the two of you are more than it would appear."

"I'll take the L.A. assignment," Morning said coolly. "Thanks a lot, Renée." She picked up the folder and began to empty out her briefcase contents onto Renée's desk. "Now if that's all settled, when do I leave for Los Angeles?"

"Today, if you can manage it."

"I'm sure I can."

Renée looked somewhat surprised. She very likely had thought she would have trouble convincing Morning to leave Carmel—and Joe Hunter's house—and Morning's ready compliance came as a pleasant shock.

Morning stayed at the Holiday Inn at Beverly Hills and the big window in her room looked out over a crisscross of highways, with an extremely strange-looking sky overhead. A heavy, pink cloud of smog seemed to be hanging, lurking, very low just over the city. It reminded her of a streak of soiled cotton candy.

Shortly after arriving, Morning went jogging and found that her throat and eyes burned so much that she hurried back to the safety of the hotel. She showered, half-listening for a call from Joe, but none came. Having washed her hair and done her nails, she realized it was absurd to leave a man—more or less—and then moon for him to phone. Either she was willing to become Joe's lover or she was not.

Right now, she was not. That, however, didn't mean she was able to stop thinking about him.

Her first meeting with Marcella Stratton was at ten the following morning. Early for New York actresses perhaps, but in California, it was considered somewhat well into the day. At the moment, Marcella was "between pictures," a phrase often used by out-of-work actors. Lately Marcella could be seen appearing in horror films, the usual slide down the ladder for stars of the silver screen who had been around for a long time.

Morning entered the restaurant exactly at ten. The place was small, somewhat dark, and was filled with men and women in expensive, casual clothes—most of them talking earnestly about "The Industry," or the making of motion pictures. A famous married actor sat at a table near the entrance. He smiled and flirted at Morning as she came in, probably from force of habit. She felt vastly uncomfortable and in that moment wished with all her heart that she were back with Joe, sitting in the kitchen, talking about anything—his house, his past. She hadn't asked him questions about his childhood. What if she never saw him again?

A waiter came up to her from the near-darkness and

asked her name. Yes. Miss Stratton was waiting. This way, please.

"I hope I didn't make you wait, Miss Stratton," Morning said, extending her hand to the seated woman. "This town has a lot of cars, all of them on that freeway, it seems."

"Not at all, my dear. Sit down, please."

The voice was husky, still lovely. Morning had more or less expected some joke of a woman, faded, hard as Renée was. Someone who married as if the married state were an addiction for her. Instead, she gazed into the lovely golden eyes that had made this woman famous. She had a few wrinkles, not many, and best of all, she exuded an unusual feeling—a kind of expectancy. She clearly thought her coming marriage was the one that was going to last forever, even though none of the last five had.

"Do you mind if I ask what part of the country you come from?" Marcella asked over their brunch. "Hardly anybody working in California comes from here, you know."

She was watching Morning with those golden, intelligent eyes. "I must say you don't seem at all like the other decorators who've fixed up my honeymoon houses."

"I can give you references—"

Marcella dimpled. When she'd first appeared on the screen, her charming, dimpled smile had caused some women to have plastic surgery to create what was then called "The Stratton Smile."

"I didn't mean that. I simply mean you're very wholesome and refreshing looking. I rather expected tight white pants, a leathery suntan and an alligator handbag."

It's going to be all right, Morning thought. Marcella

56

liked her and trusted her. For nearly an hour, they discussed some of the old Stratton films. Morning had seen some of them and liked them.

Finally, Marcella signed the check and they left to visit the chosen house.

"It's something of a wreck right now," Marcella told her from the velvet back seat of her expensive sedan. The driver, a young man who did not wear the usual deadpan face but who laughed at some of Marcella's stories as they drove along, obviously protected her as well as drove for her.

The house had once belonged to a very famous couple who had lived together and then married when scandal sniffed at their doorstep. Both were dead now. The place was filled with objets d'art that they had collected, strange old statues and hideous paintings.

"Dreadful, isn't it?" Marcella asked as they walked through the vast, damp, empty rooms. "Simply dreadful!"

"I'm afraid I have to agree with you, Miss Stratton. But I'm sure we can fix that." Morning ran a finger over some of the molding on the floor. "It's too damp in here, though. No use bringing in new drapes and floor covering until we get that problem taken care of."

Marcella had wandered onto the wide veranda that overlooked the small city of Hollywood.

"People made love in this house," Marcella said, almost to herself. "People fought and cried and a few of them even died upstairs in those bedrooms. Gilda Thornton lived here when she killed what's-his-name, her lover." She turned to face Morning. "And yet, I get no feeling at all that anyone has ever been here. I can't hear their sighs or voices or sense any presence but yours and mine. Doesn't that seem a bit odd to you? I bought this house because of its past, you know. So many famous lovers have lived under this roof that I felt it would bring good luck to Charles and me. Charles—he's my fiancé."

"It's only made of stone and glass and wood, Miss Stratton. It's only a house, after all. It can't hold onto or store the feelings and thoughts of people who once lived here. How could it?"

Marcella was watching her. "Did you say it's *only* a house?"

"Of course," Morning said. "That's all it is. Something manmade, put together with mortar and wood and all the other things they use to build houses."

"I thought decorators were supposed to *adore* houses," Marcella said, watching her. "I thought they were supposed to think of houses as people. Aren't they always saying things like—'Oh, darling—this house is really you'?"

Morning laughed. "This decorator doesn't do that, I'm afraid. I wouldn't dream of adoring a house!" Her voice was light.

But Marcella was still watching her. "Are you by any chance one of those—Christians?"

Morning's tone was still lighthearted. "Yes," she said pleasantly. "Yes, I am."

"I thought there was something weird about you," Marcella told her, but she did not sound at all displeased. "Come on—let's have a look at the weeds in the garden." She linked her arm through Morning's and they went out together.

But there was that small, fearful voice again, inside her heart. *Are you? Are you really still a Christian? Aren't you just about ready to accept Joe Hunter—on his terms? Isn't it only a question of time—a question of time—before you give in to Joe, become his lover?*

58

Every morning promptly at ten, Morning met with Marcella Stratton for brunch. Then they were driven to the house for further inspection of its crumbling rooms. On the third day, Marcella took Morning to dinner at a posh place in Malibu, not far, Morning reckoned, from Joe's beach house, the one where she'd spent that time with him five years before.

Although there were still no phone calls from Joe, who was by the end of that week somewhere on the road in concert, there were plenty of calls from Renée, who seemed to be hoping the Marcella Stratton job would bring forth a lot of other new clients. Not able to reach Morning during the day, Renée called late at night.

"I'm telling everyone in Carmel that you actually did Joe Hunter's house, darling, that the ideas were yours, which of course, they were. I'm only here to finish up loose ends while you go beautify the new house of a famous movie star."

"And do they believe that hogwash, Renée?"

"You did do the planning and got very good prices for the Hunter place," Renée told her. "Apparently, having that old beach house resemble a garden inside and out is an idea that Hunter liked. So, incidentally, does the village of Carmel. I've had five calls asking for your services, darling. And it certainly doesn't hurt us for me to tell them you'd adore working for them as soon as you finish a fabulous assignment in Hollywood!"

Morning closed her eyes. "Renée, is there something else? I have to be up early tomorrow to meet Miss Stratton for breakfast. She's changed the time from ten to eight."

"Oh? She must like you then, darling. Marvelous!"

"She's very lonely," Morning said.

"How could she be lonely, with all those ex-husbands and one victim about to become a husband before he joins the others?"

"I wasn't talking about—never mind," Morning said. "Is that all, then?"

"Just one more thing," Renée said, "have you seen the papers?"

"No." Deliberately, she had not bought them because she did not want to read about Joe's concert tour.

"The Hunter concert has been a madhouse. He changed his image overnight, they say—'back to his angry, rebellious, sexy self' it says in the *Tribune*."

"Renée, I'm really not interested."

"I may have made a serious mistake in switching you to L.A. People in Carmel are begging for you, and the firm hasn't had a single call from L.A.," Renée told her. "I think I might just say you dashed down to Los Angeles to do a quick appraisal on a house and that you were so in love with the Hunter beach house in Carmel that you begged me to—"

"Renée," Morning said steadily. "Don't, please, don't do that! I mean I—I don't see any need for my going back there and—and talking to Mr. Hunter about—anything. And I definitely am not in love with his house! So forget that idea, please."

"For now, I will, darling. But only for now."

After their early breakfast, Morning and Marcella Stratton once again visited the house Marcella had bought. This time, however, Marcella seemed unusually quiet, not at all her bubbling, about-to-be-married self.

She and Morning rode back to Morning's hotel around noon. Morning had declined the offer to have lunch, saying she really needed time to make phone calls and get some crews started working inside the house. "We haven't too much time," she told Marcella before she got out of the big car. "I want to do a good job for you, get you good prices. And that takes time."

"I hope I'm doing the right thing," Marcella said, and her golden eyes seemed childlike and frightened. "Do you know—I've only known Chuck for three months." She smiled suddenly. "I've been married so often that it seems strange to me when there isn't a man around." She patted Morning's hand. "Maybe we could talk sometime."

"Of course. Look, I'd love to have you come upstairs to the room. We could talk about what's troubling you."

"I know what's troubling me, don't I, Pete?" Marcella spoke in the direction of the driver.

He turned around and grinned like a schoolboy. "She gets married too much," he said. "Lots of those guys are after her money."

"Do you know why I keep this naughty person on my payroll?" Marcella tapped him on the head with one finger. "Because he tells the truth, darn it. He's one of those Christians too." She leaned back in the velvet seat. "I'm surrounded by weirdos!"

For a brief second, Morning's eyes met those of Pete, the driver. She smiled at him as she got out of the car.

There, she told herself as she rode up the elevator to her hotel room, *it just happened again! Another Christian suddenly appears and I feel a lot of my gloom melt away like clouds before sunshine*.

The phone in her room was flashing its small red button. Without thinking, she picked it up.

"Yes, Renée?"

"This is Joe Hunter. Please don't hang up."

Slowly, Morning sank onto the bed, kicking off her shoes. She felt as if a great burden had somehow been lifted from her.

"I'd never do that."

"But you'd run out on a good buddy. You promised never to do that again but you did it, right?"

"I'm sorry, Joe. I really am."

"Sure. People who are sorry always take off for L.A. What's your boyfriend think of all that? Doesn't he mind when you hole up in Hollywood and leave him behind?" There was a small pause. She could never tell at first, when he spoke to her in this light, teasing tone, if there was an undercurrent of seriousness. This time, however, she felt certain there was.

"We ought to talk sometime," she said. She seemed to be very good at asking people to—talk—about what was really important in life, what wonderful, clear answers could be found in the Bible. But if it came right down to it, she wasn't at all sure she could convince Joe Hunter or Marcella Stratton—two very rich and very famous people—of anything.

"How about tonight? I could meet you in San Diego and you could wait backstage until the concert is finished."

"I can't do that, Joe."

"Okay," he said. "Can't means don't-want-to, right?"

"I suppose it does, yes."

"Okay," he said finally. "Tell the guy you walk the line for that he has my admiration. I still wish you were my girl."

Tears flooded her eyes. "You—talk as if you don't think we'll see each other again," she said, hoping he wouldn't catch the slight waver in her voice. "Renée—my boss—told me I'd very likely have to come back to

Carmel and finish up your house. The real reason she took me off that assignment was...because she thought we were lovers."

"We're lovers, all right," he told her quietly. "We just never made love, that's all."

Chapter Five

The next evening, after a very tiring day of talking to various contractors on the telephone in the hotel room, Morning went down to the lobby and bought the papers.

She went out for a quick walk, papers under her arm, and stopped in a fast-food place for the salad bar. She wasn't hungry. She missed Joe. Sitting there with the untouched salad and cooling cup of coffee in front of her, she began reading the entertainment sections of all the papers she'd bought.

Renée had said that his style had changed overnight, that he'd gone from love ballads back to hard, angry rock, and apparently the result was that his fans went mad with joy. There had been a riot in San Francisco two days before and the police had to be called. His music was better, better than ever, they said.

He had the world at his feet. And yet, he was still calling her, sounding lonely and sad, in spite of his cool, joking manner.

She walked back to the hotel and was halfway across the lobby when a bellboy hurried up to her. There was a message for her. Morning opened the small paper.

"Mr. Hunter requests that you keep the magic phone number listed below. In case you wish to reach him, it is a number which will eventually get in touch with him, no matter where he is in concert."

There was no signature. The bellboy said no name had been given. Riding up to her room in the elevator, she wondered if it could have been Joe himself?

Whatever it was, whoever had called the message in—he still wasn't letting go of her.

And that made her feel much better. Somewhere, out there in that dark, scary world was Joe, alive and breathing. All she had to do was call that number, and he would get in touch.

He didn't want to lose her again.

"You look tired," Marcella Stratton told her the next morning at early breakfast near Studio City. "I hope I haven't been working you too hard."

"I'm fine, Miss Stratton, thanks. And I've got all the bid figures in. I believe this one is the best offer for the wallpapering. They're very reliable people. All you need to do is choose your patterns now. If you want to go with the country French look—"

"I'm not really sure if I want to go with anything," Marcella said suddenly. Her golden eyes met Morning's over the rim of her coffee cup. "You'll never guess what I did last night," she said. "I actually sat and listened while Pete—he's my driver—"

"Yes."

"—and his wife and two other people sat in my car and talked to me about—about some things in the Bible."

Morning smiled. "I'm so glad!"

66

"And now I'm more confused than ever," Marcella said. "What were you saying about wallpaper?"

Suddenly, Morning put her hand on Marcella's, covering, for a moment, the huge diamond engagement ring. "There isn't really a big rush, is there, Miss Stratton? I mean, we could still go ahead with the house but maybe you might like some time—to think about your personal situation."

"Study the Bible. That's what you mean, isn't it?"

"Yes."

Marcella very nearly dimpled. "You weirdos have a certain way about you. Did you know that?"

For the rest of the day, Morning busied herself getting wallpaper samples together and checking them against the paint colors to show Marcella.

It crossed Morning's mind that God had sent her here to do something much more important than decorate Marcella's house.

That evening, she phoned Marcella's house, using an unpublished number Marcella had given her the day before. It was Pete who answered.

"She's gone to Mexico," he told Morning. "She said she wanted to get some sun and think."

"Oh," she said hesitantly.

"It's just for a week," he told her. "Look, we're having Bible study here tonight. Miss Stratton lets us use the recreation room for study anytime we want. Would you like to come over?"

"Yes, thank you, I would, very much."

Pete gave her the address, and on the way, in the taxi, another thought, crystal clear, came to Morning.

What if Marcella is trying to run from God? From His love for her?

Morning knew about that kind of running. She'd been doing quite a lot of it herself lately.

67

She left the Bible study with the same feeling as always—as if she'd put on a nearly forgotten cloak that warmed her, helped her get through each day.

But back in her room it was only a matter of hours before she found herself giving in to the impulse to call Joe and talk to him. She sat in front of the phone with a feeling of excitement. He had said this was the magic phone number. But what would she say to him? Tonight—she had made a mental note of his schedule—he would be in Denver.

She dialed the number. It rang four times and a somewhat familiar voice answered. Instead of saying hello, he simply repeated the number she had dialed.

"Hello," Morning said steadily, "I—I was given this number and I'd like to speak with Mr. Joe Hunter, please."

Surprisingly, there was no questioning, no screening.

"I'll ring his number," the voice told her. It was neither cordial nor rude, just doing the job. "When you get through to that number, I'll hang up. So wait until you hear me hang up before you start to talk. Mr. Hunter," he said, "likes his privacy."

"Yes," Morning said, getting a trifle nervous, "I'll do that."

What followed was a series of strange clicking noises. Then a silence. She thought they must have been cut off when suddenly, there was Joe's voice, weary, tough-sounding, gruff.

"Yeah?"

"Joe?"

He let his breath out in what sounded like a long sigh. Then: "I don't believe this. I can't believe you decided to get in touch!" But he was clearly glad. "You didn't just call me to tell me something I don't want to hear about, did you? Like about that house in Carmel?"

She smiled. He always had been completely open about his feelings for her.

"This isn't a business call," she said.

"Okay," he said quickly. "Okay. Now we've got to make plans to be together again—really together. Where are you?"

"Joe, I didn't call to—"

"Honey," he said, "where are you?"

"I'm in Los Angeles."

"Good. I'll send a plane for you, my private plane. I'll meet you at the Denver airport—no—wait I'll have to send a car. I have to do a late show tonight—"

"Joe, I don't see how I can do that! I only called you to tell you I miss you. Just that." She swallowed, feeling as if she might have made another mistake with him. Sending a car, sending a jet plane—was that what she really wanted in her life? The idea of a private jet, a car waiting at an airport, and Joe onstage someplace bothered her. Somehow, she didn't want to be the one to go running to him.

"I can't cancel out here," he said suddenly. "Just—not show up. My music is too important to too many people. Listen, you stay where you are in L.A. and I'll be there in time for—"

"Joe, do you remember, five years ago, when we—when we were at your house in Malibu and I told you I wanted to make love with you but I wasn't going to because of my beliefs? I told you then that I'm a Christian, and that making love before marriage would be wrong for me. God doesn't want that for His people."

"And," Joe asked quietly, "do you remember that I countered all of that by my own very important question?"

69

"Yes," she said softly.

"I asked you to marry me, Morning. I meant it then—and I mean it now."

She could scarcely speak. "I think we'd better talk," she said. "Could you do your concert and come here, do you think?"

"Hold breakfast," he said warmly. "I'll leave Denver right after the final show."

"Joe—"

"Like I said, sweetheart—hold breakfast for me!"

"Goodnight," she told him, and she hung up. Done. She'd be with him once again, in the morning. Was this, then, the kind of "joy...in the morning" the Bible spoke of? Or was she only blindly prolonging her own sorrow over finally giving him up—because she couldn't share him with those screaming fans he sang to?

Awake very early, Morning planned to jog. As she dressed, she tucked her Bible into the pocket of her running slacks. Along the way, she stopped, took some deep breaths, and sat on a bench near a bus stop. It seemed an odd place to open her Bible, but as soon as she began to read, she forgot where she was. The words—familiar yet always fresh for her need, like some stunning puzzle to be worked out by grace—filled her mind and came into her heart.

What if she could keep her faith, have her need for God fulfilled, and still have Joe and his sweet human love?

Was that possible?

And she remembered: "With God all things are possible." Jesus had said that. Of course. Just because it didn't *seem* possible didn't mean He wouldn't make it that way!

A little flicker of hope, like an ever-burning candle, rekindled inside her. God, through Christ, had given her that most priceless of human needs. She now dared to hope—for herself and Joe.

Morning had returned to her room and was pulling off her blue velour suit when the phone rang.

"You should be having early breakfast with Marcella," Renée challenged her, "shouldn't you?"

"Marcella has gone to Mexico," Morning said, looking somewhat anxiously toward the bathroom, where the tub water was running. "She'll be gone a week, Renée."

"What? Getting a divorce so soon? I thought she was going to marry this one *after* you finished their honeymoon cottage!"

"She didn't go there to divorce anybody, Renée. She went there to think."

"Don't be absurd, darling. People like that never *think*! They just *do*. Get married, get divorced, get their names in the rag papers. By the way, I've got some information on the Hunter beach house for you."

"Oh?" Morning very nearly smiled. What, she wondered, would Renée, who—in spite of her personal life—kept a spotless moral reputation for the firm she represented, think and do if she knew Joe Hunter was on his way here at this very moment? "What sort of information, Renée?"

"He's changed his mind about the central theme."

"What? Are you saying he doesn't like the garden theme?" Joe had loved it when she'd presented it to him. He had said it was a lovely idea, bringing a garden indoors the way she wanted to—

"I don't understand it either, darling. Now he wants

71

it—well, the best way I can think to describe it is—funky."

"Funky!" Impossible. That meant Ugly Hollywood. It meant the punk-rock look, the electronic, cheap, vulgar look that so many Hollywood people were spending small fortunes to bring into their homes. "Are you sure Joe Hunter wants—"

"I'm sure he was advised by his business manager or somebody," Renée told her. "This look goes along with the new songs he's been doing. Haven't you heard about that, darling? They say he's full of rage or something. People adore that. They think it's sexy. Anyway, it all means more money for us, of course, since he first approved one decorating look and now he's changed his mind."

"Joe wouldn't change his mind in that way," Morning said, but she knew he would. He could change his music, change his songs and his houses too, but what about the core of him, the essence of him? Wasn't that person dear and decent, yearning, needing love, willing to give back just as much love, as long as the girl in his life stayed close to him?

"I believe I heard you call him 'Joe' again," Renée said, her voice alert and cold. "I told you not ever to call him—"

"I'll have to get back to you, Renée," Morning said quickly. There was a soft knocking on her hotel room door. Polite. No, it wouldn't be Joe. He didn't do things that way. Joe would have to make his own kind of entrance, not with bells and a big crowd, but in some other distinctive, delightful way. "I'll get back to you."

"Keep me up on Marcella Stratton's house," Renée told her. "I'm not sure I can handle all of this—Hunter deciding he wants a different look, Marcella Stratton going to Mexico all of a sudden—"

"Goodby, Renée." Morning hung up and hurried to turn off the water before answering the door.

It was the same bellboy, smiling happily. He'd probably just been given an enormous tip.

"I have a message," he announced. "Mr. J. H. wants you to meet him at the second garbage can just off the—ah—east exit."

"He—*what*?"

"Be glad to show you the way, ma'am."

"Please wait in the hall for a moment."

When he agreed, she closed the door and quickly finished dressing. She sighed as she opened the drain in the tub. She had been looking forward to a luxurious bath. She checked herself in the mirror and then opened the door to the waiting bellboy.

She grabbed her purse and briefcase, handed the young man her suitcase, and followed him down the hallway, to the elevators, and on around the corner of the building.

"Wait," she said suddenly, and the bellboy turned and looked at her politely. Morning went up to him. "Look. I'm very sorry, but I don't think this is a good idea at all."

"Well," he said, "all I know is that—I'm not supposed to say who, but—"

"Would you mind telling me where Mr. Hunter plans to meet me?"

"Just around there," he told her, "by the east kitchen. They wanted him to have bacon and eggs in the kitchen, I think. I mean, it isn't every day that a big country-rock star comes wandering into the hotel by the kitchen door."

"Okay," Morning said. "Which garbage can, then? Assuming he's had his bacon and eggs."

A grin on the bellboy's face caused her to look to the left.

Joe was lounging against the building, obviously waiting for her. A small cluster of people from the kitchen seemed to be waiting too.

"Hey," a boy in a chef's high hat yelled, "she's coming—is that the one?"

For answer, Joe came to her and soundly kissed her, then smiled at the small cheering crowd. "My compliments," he told them, "to the chefs. Best bacon, best eggs I've had the pleasure of wolfing down since I left Memphis. And thanks for not telling the world that this lovely lady and I are about to get into a car and drive away. If you weren't all so nice—we'd probably have somebody with a camera here by now."

"Have a nice day," somebody said, to let them know that nobody was going to call the tabloids.

His car, or one of them, was parked around the corner. It was an old coupe of some kind, with a rumble seat, and it looked in perfect condition. The engine sounded new.

"Sorry about breakfast," he said, pulling into the stream of traffic. "But I'll eat another one if you'll just tell me what kind of place you like best."

"Anyplace you like," she told him.

He reached for her hand, holding it briefly to his lips. "I booked several places," he told her, the light dancing in his blue eyes. "Aspen. I know a guy there with a ski-house and it's empty for the next week. How does that sound?"

"Joe, I'm not—I never said I—" her voice broke off. Was she spoiling it already? Was she spoiling this precious little time of theirs by insisting that his every suggestion was wrong?

"Look," he said quietly, his voice kind, "I want you

to know something about me, honey—something important. I'm not going to do anything to—make you leave me. Just remember that. And I don't go around asking women to marry me very often. As a matter of fact—"

She had impulsively leaned over and kissed his face, right on the nice crease in his cheek.

"Mmmmm," he murmured. "I just thought of a wonderful place," he said.

"Joe, I can't go to somebody's lodge with you and—you know what might happen! You know," she said almost desperately, "what *would* happen!"

He grinned, looking for a brief instant into her eyes.

"Sure I do," he said. "But at the moment, the wonderful place I'm thinking of happens to be a little diner over off Wilshire. I think I can handle more bacon and eggs, if you promise to eat a nice, nourishing breakfast. Okay?"

She leaned her head against his shoulder. "Oh," she said, as she just gave in to being loved and looked after, "I think I might be able to force myself!"

But as they sat at the long counter in the diner, the waitress set their plates of eggs and potatoes and bacon in front of them and without glancing at them went straight to the pay phone.

Joe suddenly grabbed Morning's hand.

"Got to go, honey," he told her, his voice low. "We'll eat someplace else."

"But—Joe—" she had a piece of jellied toast in one hand. She grabbed her purse and let him hurry her out to his car. She turned to look at him as he got behind the wheel.

"Don't tell me," she said. "Herds of female fans were about to stampede the place." She made her voice light, but something was bothering her.

"Wrong. That little squealie behind the counter was calling somebody—everybody in L.A. knows somebody with a camera. I just don't want us to be plastered all over one of those rag sheets, that's all." He glanced at her. "I'm sorry, baby. We'll find a nice, safe place where we can have breakfast without being bothered."

But was there such a place?

"Joe," she told him. "I'm really not all that hungry. I think we ought to go back to your house. I really think that's where we ought to go to talk—"

Joe steered the car toward the desert highway from L.A. back to Carmel. Breakfast, they decided, could wait for a while.

In Salinas, Joe stopped and made a phone call from a booth, while Morning got Cokes from the machine and went to the women's room. Her face, she noticed as she washed up, looked flushed and happy and somehow childlike. *Careful*, she told herself. *Remember that Joe Hunter isn't a Christian.*

Joe was leaning against the side of his car, waiting for her.

"About twenty people are out at the house," he told her. "They're busy decorating it. I told them to clear out, but they say by the time they get their stuff together it'll be maybe an hour. I was thinking of you and me and a swim and then a feast by the fire."

"It doesn't really matter," she told him, putting on her sunglasses. "I'm just glad you've changed your mind again."

"About what? Not about us," he said, and he kissed the tip of her nose, just below where the glasses had slid. "Never about us, Morning."

"I was thinking more along the lines of those people

76

who are doing your house with pictures of snakes and bilious colors."

"So your boss—what's-her-name—"

"Renée."

"Told you. Okay, I was mad. When I feel like that—when someone I love leaves, I feel that kind of outrage. Like when my brother died."

She touched his cheek gently.

"You don't need to feel that way ever again. All you have to do is—" Her courage was failing. She wanted with all her heart to be strong, sure of saying the right things, the perfect words, that would turn Joe Hunter around and help him choose to be a Christian.

"I know a place," he said suddenly. "He'll shut down for us—we'll have the whole restaurant to ourselves!" He started the engine. "What's more, the food there is great!"

I should have said something, something right for the moment, she thought. *What's wrong—am I ashamed to be a Christian? Ashamed to say I belong to God through Christ—and I want Joe to follow that road too?*

She didn't know. Oh, how she wished with all her heart that she could think just of this sweet, wonderful time at hand, here with Joe beside her. She could look at his dear face and see him quickly glance at her, eyes blue and happy, and she could reach and lightly touch his hand with hers. They were, in these past few hours, closer than ever before.

A week. He had spoken of their taking a week together, and Marcella Stratton would be in Mexico for a week. *After all, I could be working on Joe's house, and I'd tell him then. Then I'll find the right words.*

Chapter Six

"I think," Morning told him from her lounge chair on the deck facing the sea, "I hear a telephone ringing, Joe."

"Probably somebody wanting to buy the house," he said.

They were holding hands at sunset, having had a long swim and the long-awaited breakfast. (Morning had declined his idea of renting an entire restaurant so they wouldn't be noticed.) Soon after their arrival she had spent a good two hours on the telephone, getting the wallpaper-and-paint people to start work on the house. Joe had agreed to use the original idea of bringing a garden inside the old house and landscaping the entire grounds to enhance the effect.

"Joe, you really ought to answer it."

He was kissing her hair, but when she gently pushed him away he reluctantly went to answer the screeching telephone. Morning gazed out over the calm Pacific. She was happy. That realization came to her with a lovely clarity. She was happy!

She had not experienced happiness—or a form of it—for such a long time that she didn't quite recognize the feeling. It was a mixture of excitement and joy and an odd sense of peace whenever she was near him.

They had nearly a week, six and one-half beautiful days, to look forward to.

She still wasn't certain how things would go. Joe's housekeeper had come in for the week, so it would all be "proper," and she'd do most of the cooking. From one of the sparsely furnished bedrooms, Morning could continue with her work on the house. In the evenings, she and Joe could go swimming or walk on the beach. And she had promised herself that one night soon, when they were together and their day was finished, she would talk to him of Jesus.

But she had no idea what to say or how to say it. Christianity simply did not fit in with Joe's lifestyle. How could it? He lived in a tightly secured world of endless money, adoring women, and men who tried to please him because he paid them well. His music and songs reflected his moods, and no matter how he felt or what he wrote, his fans wanted him. There might conceivably come a point in his career when he no longer had to be young or entertaining to hold his fans. The music was the magic.

Even now someone apparently was trying to get him to go back to work much sooner than planned. Joe was talking on the phone, something about the tour. Something about Chicago and a lot of advance ticket sales. She closed her eyes. Joe was polite but firm. Then his voice seemed to harden. Clearly he did not like to be told what he ought to do. Finally, he slammed down the phone with such a bang that Morning's half-closed eyes flew open. Joe strode back onto the deck and stood at the railing, not saying anything, clearly furious.

"I'm going to have to go to Chicago," he said, his voice edged with bitterness. "Or get sued."

"Joe, of course you should go!"

Still, he didn't look at her. "But I don't want to leave you," he said quietly. "Having you here with me—I'd given up thinking this would happen."

Stella, the housekeeper who had moved in for the week, along with her two dogs, ambled to the deck barefooted, to tell them dinner was ready. For the moment that eased the strain between them.

The meal was not fussy or elegant, but hearty. They had a stew of fresh Carmel-valley-grown vegetables in a flavorful sauce, fresh bread from the oven and a fine pecan pie. Mr. Hunter, the housekeeper said, was partial to Southern-type desserts.

Then they went to enjoy the fire that was laid in the living room.

Joe's anger had mellowed to grim resolution and regret when he brought up the subject of the concert again.

"It's only that one-night concert at Newtown," he said, as they sat before the fire after dinner.

Morning sat with her long, tanned legs stretched out and crossed before the fire. She wore cut-off jeans and one of Joe's tee shirts. She felt warmed and wonderful.

"You must go, Joe. You don't want a lot of trouble. Besides," she told him, "it's only one night."

"One day and all night, honey. Chicago isn't just across the street. Even if I have Dave fly me there in my plane, I still won't be back for twenty-four hours."

She closed her eyes. "We've got time."

"Sure. Sure we have." His gentle hand cupped her chin, tilting it upward, so that when she opened her eyes she must look at him. She felt his lips lightly kiss her closed lids, and then slowly, she opened her eyes. His intense, tender blue gaze made her heart reel.

"I'm sorry," he said quietly. "I didn't want to have to leave you—ever."

She gave herself to the kiss, the closeness, the warmth and strength of him. Tears slid down her cheeks. When he realized this he kissed the tears, whispering her name.

Suddenly, he pulled away from her. He was listening, and in that instant Morning heard it too—some human sound, low, hushed—laughing! No, giggling—out on the deck. Someone was watching them!

Morning stood up, fury washing over her as Joe strode quickly to the glass door, opened it, and grabbed someone. There was a delighted squeal from the female victim.

Then he escorted inside two young girls who couldn't have been over fourteen or fifteen. He scolded them like a big brother.

"You can call your parents to come and get you, but if I ever see the two of you around here again, I'll call the local cops—no kidding. I might have shot you or something."

They didn't believe he'd do that. One of them giggled and the other seemed about to faint with awe.

"I think I'll go work on the house plans," Morning said, excusing herself. She went upstairs. Moments later she heard more conversation—Joe's voice, gentle and kind, and the girls' prattle sounded slightly hysterical. Finally, she heard a car in front and then more conversation. The parents were probably big fans of Joe's too.

It was now dark outside, going on ten. Morning had stretched out on the bed finally, wishing she could finish the work she'd spoken of, but she couldn't set her mind to it. It was not that she was jealous of those silly children downstairs. It was simply that they were the handwriting on the wall, so to speak. The handwriting on her wall.

There would be no escaping this sort of thing if she were to marry Joe. He had asked her to marry him—or had he? He certainly hadn't talked about any plans since they'd gotten back to his house.

He tapped at her door, and at her quick "come in," he opened it, looking somewhat sheepish.

"They just left," he said.

"Yes. I heard the car."

He came in and sat next to her on the narrow bed. "You okay?"

"Of course," she said somewhat stiffly. "Why shouldn't I be?"

"That—doesn't happen often," he said, and then, meeting her eyes, he got up and went over to the window. "Okay. It happens a lot. I don't like it, but I don't really want to get tough about it. They—they're only kids," he said.

"Joe, it's all right!"

"Another thing—since I'm holding off on five days' work on the tour, I promised my manager I'd do a recording session so the guys in the group don't get rusty. I don't have to—"

"Joe, I think we'd better get something straight," she said suddenly. "We can't try to hide from the world this way."

"I told you, it's just that one trip to Chicago and—"

"This isn't going to work, Joe!" She felt so sorry for him, for them, now that she'd said the words. "We're—you and I are trying to recapture that week we had together in another time and place. Don't you see that?"

"What I don't see," he replied somewhat peevishly, "is anything wrong with that. Look, I deal with the so-

83

called world—people after me for money, people after me to hire them, to listen to their songs, to record my songs, to get up on a stage or get on a plane—all the time. That's what the world is like when music is what you do. And frankly, I don't get a lot of pleasure out of it."

"Maybe pleasure isn't what you should be looking for," she said quietly. "Maybe that's what's all wrong about us, Joe. Looking for pleasure. Running away from the world so we can live some kind of a seven-day dream, just the two of us. We've hardly begun," she said softly, "and already we can tell it just isn't going to work."

He was looking at her. "Marry me," he said suddenly. "We'll pack a couple of suitcases, get in the Jeep, and go down to Nashville and get married. We can sit out the waiting period in a condo I keep there. I'll even take Mrs. what's-her-name—Stella—if you want everything to be—"

'Joe, I don't think that's a very good idea."

His tanned face seemed to pale with some emotion.

"Okay. Then what *do* you think is a good idea?"

He was angry with her. Disappointed. Or thought he was.

"Joe, I really don't think you want to marry me."

"I don't ask people to marry me when I don't mean it." He shook his head. "What I mean is—I've never thought much about it. Morning, all I know is I can't make it without you, and if that means marriage, okay."

"What about—the way I feel about—"

"Okay. So you're a Christian. That's great, honey! My mother would have given us her blessing because she wanted me to marry a—"

"Nice girl? A good girl?"

84

"Sure. Sure she did." But he looked uncomfortable.

"Then why are you afraid?" She got up and went closer to him. "Why are you afraid of the idea of our getting married, if you're so sure it's the right thing to do?" She was pinning him down unmercifully. "Could it be that you're afraid I might change your lifestyle? Make wifely demands about your crazy fans and your mean music and the way people who listen to you react? That I might even say you have a responsibility to those people and to lead them down the wrong road with your music and songs is wrong?" Her voice was husky with feeling. "And that it might cause you to lose your eternal life with God?"

His eyes were level. "If you mean do I want a wife who'll tell me how to run my life, the answer is no. I couldn't handle that, I'm the boss." He smiled at her, trying to lighten up their conversation. "But I'm a very nice boss, and I'm so in love with you that I'm willing to try…if you are." He was waiting, waiting for her to give him an answer. The moment of truth had arrived.

"I love you, Joe," she said, nearly whispering, "but I couldn't live this life. I just couldn't!"

"You want me to quit? Is that it?"

"No! I…I'm not sure what I want! I mean—"

"What? What's holding us back, Morning?"

"We need Christ," she said. She took a deep breath. "He can change things for us, make things right that seem so impossible to us—"

Joe's eyes changed, deepened. A look of worry came into them.

"I'm not…I haven't been—" He looked away from her. "In this business, you run into a lot of slime," he said. "Maybe I should have kicked a lot of it away from my door. But I didn't, not always."

85

"That doesn't matter, Joe. He's very good at forgiving."

"Morning...I can't just walk away from all of this! My work, my music. You can't expect me to do that!" There was a distinct edge to his voice. "Not even you," he said, "can expect me to do that."

There was a silence. Finally, she went to him and put her arms around him. His tall body felt rigid from anger, from wanting her, from worrying about what she expected of him.

"What about your recording session?"

"What?"

"Aren't you supposed to record someplace tonight? You said—"

"It's set up for Monterey," he told her. "We rented a studio. So I won't be late. At least I don't have to go to San Francisco or L.A. to get it done."

"That's good." She nestled her head against his shoulder. "Joe?" As if they had a will of their own, his arms slowly went around her until she stood in the warm circle of his embrace.

"Let's not fight," he said against her ear. "Honey—"

"Let me go with you. Maybe I can learn something about your work, your life." *Maybe I can learn to stand living your kind of lifestyle.*

He seemed delighted at the idea of her going to the recording studio with him. Morning went to her room, took a quick shower, and put on a skirt, low heels, and a fresh blouse. She hoped she looked nice but not prudish. She bought most of her clothes in San Francisco, paid enough for them so that they would last, usually got well-made things that were color coordinated, and let it go at that.

"You smell like soap," Joe told her as they pulled out of the driveway in his Jeep. "Remember, if any of the guys gives you a look—" he glanced at her as they headed toward Highway One. "Do you know what kind of look I mean?"

Morning smiled. "I think you mean leer, not look."

He laughed, putting her small hand under his on the steering wheel. "Once they know you're mine," he told her, "they won't dare."

Once they know you're mine.

But was she really?

Morning sat in the sound booth somewhat uncomfortably, but Joe had insisted she be there, saying he wanted her opinion. It did no good at all for her to tell him she wasn't an expert on music; he wanted her there. When they finally got set up, with the back-up people behind him and three pretty girl singers on his right, at another mike, the first try began. It was one of his most loved songs, "All My Hungry Yesterdays," and he sang it right to—and obviously for—Morning. Her heart warmed with pride. The three girl singers cast glances at her from time to time, and Morning saw them in a little circle whispering between "takes," but she didn't mind. If Joe didn't want her here, she wouldn't be here. Simple as that.

They worked on a newer song, "Won't You Say Yes?" and midway through there was a long discussion about "delivery."

"I think that's a mistake, Joe," the producer, a man in a white shirt and loose tie and black-rimmed glasses said, speaking from the glass booth. "After the way they reacted when you did that one in Nashville—"

"I've decided to change the delivery," Joe said quietly.

"They like it when you're mad, Joe," the man said,

keeping his voice good-natured. "Try it that way just one time, okay?"

"Toby," Joe said patiently, "I just told you. I'm not doing the number that way. Period."

The man named Toby glanced suspiciously at the corner where Morning sat, silent and waiting.

"They won't like it, baby," he said to Joe. "They want you sad and mad, the madder the—"

"How would you like to go on home and forget about being my producer, Toby?"

"Okay," he said. "Sure. One more time, folks. Try it from the top, please—"

Midway through the number Toby turned to Morning.

"Want to do him a favor, Miss?"

She did *not* like this man. He clearly didn't want her there and he seemed intent on trying to get Joe to continue with the kind of music she found so wrong for him. The kind of music he wrote and sang and played when he was full of hurt and misery.

"That depends," she said calmly, "on whether or not Joe wants the favor done for him."

"This is the kind of favor we don't tell him about," he said evenly. "The kind that's real good for his career."

"If it's good for his career, Joe ought to know about it," she said. "Besides, I don't have much say about his career."

"The two of you aren't exactly serious, you mean?"

"I mean it's none of your business."

She felt a bit shocked at her own boldness. How could she have talked that way? Well, maybe it was time she learned a bit about Joe's kind of people, the ones who walked around in his own particular world.

Moments later, when they were making some

88

changes on "Lovin' Won't Be the Same with Her," Toby came over and sat next to Morning.

"I wanted to mention a party," he said, smiling. He was perhaps thirty-five, one of the many youngish men who worked around and for Joe. He looked well-fed, tanned, and relaxed. Morning wondered if Joe had made him rich. He very likely had.

"You're talking to the wrong person," she said. "Sorry."

"It's a Carmel party, honey. Given in Joe's honor. If he could just drop by it'd look good for him. These people, they have a lot of clout. You'd be surprised at the names they can drop."

"Really? Well I'm afraid you'll have to tell this to Joe," Morning said, "because I only came along to watch."

His hand suddenly snaked out and grabbed her wrist. He didn't hurt her, but his fingers were firm. "I can help you," he told her. "Do you sing by any chance?"

"If you don't take your hand away," Morning said steadily, "I'm going to start screaming."

The moist hand flew from her wrist. "No harm intended," he told her. "I'm only looking after Joe's best interests."

Morning said nothing more to him. She thought about telling Joe, but decided against it. He might become furious, overreact, and fire the man.

They did the number again. It was a "take," and Joe headed for the glass booth. He ignored Toby.

"Ready to go, Morning?"

"Yes." She gathered up her sweater and purse.

"I introduced you and Toby, didn't I?" Joe asked.

"Sure you did," Toby said, trying to smile. "The lady sure does have a pretty name."

"Well, remember it," Joe told him. "And pass the word: This lady is my fiancée."

On the ride back, he glanced at her worriedly.

"You okay?"

"Of course." She was huddled down in the seat. "I'm not sure I understood what the argument was about, but I'd say they want you to give the fans a wilder image—leather and lights, I think the man said."

"Toby? He just likes money. Did he mention a party to you?"

"Yes." She hoped he wouldn't ask too many questions. Her wrist still burned from those thick, moist fingers.

"A guy who has a restaurant in Carmel—tough movie star type—wants me to do a film with him." He laughed. "Can you imagine me as an actor?"

She could indeed. Women would love seeing him on the giant screen.

"Joe," she said carefully, "it's not good for you to give things up just because you think I won't—fit in."

"If you don't belong there," he told her, "then neither do I."

She didn't believe that, and, of course, he didn't either. There was also the matter of his surprise announcement, calling her his "fiancée." Word would surely get around—and it simply was not true. But this wasn't the time to argue over that.

"Will you go to Chicago with me, Morning? We'll only be gone for one day and night. I don't want to go without you."

"How on earth would I explain *that* to Renée?"

"Don't," he told her. "Don't explain anything to anybody." He found her hand and pressed it to his warm lips.

Joe usually left the iron gates leading to the beach house open, and they were that way tonight. Halfway down the lane that led to the circular front driveway, he and Morning saw the cars parked in front of the house. There were six or seven of them, and a lot of people were milling around on the deck.

"Guys from my band," Joe said, his voice low and threaded with displeasure. "Don't worry, I'll get rid of them."

The band and several women, including the back-up singers, had invaded the beach house. Toby was among them. He was the first to get to Joe's side when Joe parked. Morning stayed put.

"If you won't come to the party," Toby said, smiling, holding a glass in one hand and a bottle of champagne in the other, "the party comes to you, buddy!"

"I thought I told you I wasn't in the mood, Toby," Joe said quietly. "Look, I don't want to be a—" he glanced at Morning, not wanting to use the word in front of her, "but I thought I made it clear that I didn't want any of this. Not tonight. So if you'll just take your ladies and get out of here—"

Two women suddenly pushed forward and stood boldly in front of Joe.

"Can I kiss you?" one asked, her voice slightly slurred.

"Better not," Joe told her politely, "I hate kisses."

"He's kidding, isn't he?" And she threw herself upon him, pushing her mouth against his. Joe pushed her away, and Morning saw that he was really furious.

Suddenly, a bright light flashed, then another, out of the darkness.

"You brought the press here too? Toby, I'm giving you sixty seconds to get these people out of here, understand?"

"No need to get mad, Joe-baby. Cool down!" Toby was still smiling. "Your lady there—she wouldn't mind if we just make a toast to you, inside your house, would she?"

"Sixty seconds." His face was ashen under the tan.

"Joe—" Morning went to him and reached for his hand. "It's—if you don't mind—I don't." She looked at him, wanting this terrible anger in him to cease. "It's okay," she told him.

He was silent. People seemed to be swarming up the steps to the main deck. There was a lot of laughter and giggling. The doors were open and from inside the house, lights went on. Morning saw the housekeeper coming down the deck steps wearing her bathrobe. Her hair was in curlers and her dogs ran around everywhere, yapping at ankles. It was a madhouse.

"I'm sorry, Mr. Hunter," she said, "I told them they couldn't come in when you weren't here. And now that you're here—looks like they came in."

"It's okay, Stella. You go on to bed," Joe told her. "I'll get rid of them."

Morning followed him up the steps to the glass doors, which were flung open. Someone had gone to the rehearsal room and turned on the stereo. The wild, electronic music of one of Joe's "bad-man" numbers roared through the house. One of the women tossed off her shoes and then her jacket and began to dance alone in the center of the room. She was darkly beautiful, and as she danced, she stared at Joe.

More people began arriving. Somebody—probably Toby—had made phone calls saying the party had been moved to Joe's beach house. A lot of the guests were film people. It was fairly easy to tell them from the music scene group, the ones who had strange hairstyles and outlandish clothes. It began to look as if the party would go on for hours.

When Joe was suddenly called to the phone, Morning stood with a piece of cold pizza and a glass of ginger ale, pretending to enjoy watching all those people dance. Secretly, she wished they'd go. She didn't feel very comfortable with his friends.

"It isn't so bad, is it?" a man's voice asked from behind her. She turned quickly, nearly spilling the ginger ale. It was Toby.

"It's Joe's house," she told him. "It's up to him to decide about parties."

"So you and Joey are getting married! Is that for real or is he just trying to keep the guys away from you?"

Morning turned to look at this man. "Leave us alone," she said clearly. "Just leave Joe and me alone, please."

His eyes were cold behind his glasses. "Beg pardon?"

"We don't—have much time," she said. "Just leave us alone and don't make things so difficult for Joe, please."

He stirred his drink with a little stick and watched her.

"What's that supposed to mean?"

"I have to go back to Los Angeles before long and I—I'd like to get my work on this house done before I leave."

"Wait a minute—" he was staring at her. "Hey—I know who you are! I heard about you. You're from San Francisco and you got hired to fix up this place so Joe can sell it, right?" He smiled, obviously relieved. "Okay, okay—now it all comes together. I couldn't connect you with this scene, that's all."

"You don't have to."

"So you came here to fix up this house and Joe saw

93

you and decided he wanted to—be nice to you, right?"

When she started to move away from him he followed her toward the deck, but this time he didn't try to grab her or touch her in any way.

"Honey," he told her, "I just want you to know that if you want to last around here, you've got to kind of groove in with Joe's scene. And you see, doll, we're a part of his scene."

Morning took a small breath, facing him. She put down the cold pizza slice on its paper plate and set the untouched glass of ginger ale beside it, there on one of the redwood tables on the deck.

"Do you always do this?"

"What?"

"Do you always try to run Joe's life this way? Because if I were to tell him that you're bothering me, he'd fire you."

"Maybe, maybe not. I've done a lot for that boy, you know. In case you don't read the papers—"

"I read the papers."

"I'm the guy who discovered Joey Hunter in Memphis. He was working a honky-tonk joint, and he had an old guy playing piano for him, some old coot about seventy. That was it—Joe and the old guy. Joe wanted to keep that old buzzard with him—he'd still have him in the back-up except that the old guy had a stroke. So now he and his old wife get a fat check and sit in a new house in Nashville. They've got it made, thanks to Joe. The boy is a fool about money."

"Joe," Morning said evenly, "isn't a boy. He's a man, and he isn't a fool, either. He knows what kind of music is best for him and for the kids who love him. He knows that."

"But *I* know what kind of music brings in the money." His voice was hard. "He has to be mean, lean, mad, and sexy. He has to make every woman and girl in the audience dream about—"

"That's enough," Morning said, her voice low.

He stepped slightly in front of her, blocking her way.

"Just don't try to tell my boy what kind of songs to sing," he said quietly. "Or you won't even finish out the week with him, believe me!"

"Get out of my way, please," she said coolly. She looked into those hard eyes. "For your information, I intend to do everything in my power to influence Joe's music—and his life, if I can—away from that kind of sound and from the feelings and thoughts that make that sound possible. You can't hurt us. You can't break us up, even if you try!"

"Wait and see, honey," he told her. "Just wait and see."

Morning hurried back into the other room. Joe was standing with a group of people who were all talking earnestly to him. One of them was the tall, tough-guy actor Joe had mentioned earlier, the one who wanted Joe to do a film with him.

As soon as he saw her, Joe left the group and came to her.

"I thought maybe you'd left. I was about to take off and head down the beach, looking for you."

"I'm fine," she told him. She realized she was furious, but she felt very strong indeed. "I'm just fine, Joe."

"You'll be surprised at how quickly I can get rid of these people. I'm giving them another half hour and that's it. In the meantime, let's slip out through the kitchen to the back deck."

Someone, probably on Joe's orders, had put on a different tape, a love song, one of his most famous ones, called "Love Shadows." They could hear it softly wafting through the house. Joe took her in his arms and she melted into him. Her face rested against his chest and she could hear his heartbeat under her cheek. It was as if she and Joe were alone in their own place, enclosed by the sweet sounds of a love song he had written long ago for her.

"I want to kiss you," he whispered, "but somebody will take our picture if I do." He looked down at her with those beautiful eyes. "I'm in love with you, Morning."

Her own heart had begun to pound wildly.

"Joe," she whispered, "do you really want to marry me?"

"You won't believe this," he said, his mouth warm against her ear, "but I never asked anybody that before. Not unless you want to count my third-grade teacher. I asked her, but she turned me down. She's still in Mississippi and I still send her a Valentine every year."

Morning found herself wondering how many people Joe had befriended, how many needy people, like the old piano player who'd suffered the stroke, he sent checks to and looked after and bought houses for.

His hand was pressed against her back. His arms had gone tighter around her.

"I want to marry you in Nashville," he said. "That's where my folks got married. Nobody has to know. We can leave in the morning and—"

Wait, she thought. *Please—wait!*

"Honey?" The song had ended. Joe tilted her face so that she had to meet his level blue gaze. "Do you want to?"

"Yes. Yes, I do. But first I have to—we have to—"

"Okay," he said warmly. "I won't push you. Not as long as I can count on your being my girl. But you'll go with me to Chicago, won't you?"

How could she say no?

True to his word, Joe gave the order in thirty minutes and everyone left in surprisingly quick order, probably because Joe and Morning had disappeared to the dark beach, where they sat on the still-warm sand hearing cars start and drive away. Then, the last light inside the house went out, and finally the light in the housekeeper's bedroom went out too.

"Want to swim? It's nice in the water this time of night."

"Not," she told him, "without my bathing suit, which happens to be in San Francisco. And I don't want to wear one of your girlfriends', thank you."

He nuzzled his face against her neck. "I might as well quit trying to get you to do all that naughty stuff," he said, teasing her, "because you just aren't gonna do it."

She stroked his warm face. "Not until we're married. Then, just wait!"

For answer, he pushed her down onto the sand and kissed her face, her cheeks, eyes, nose, lips, ears—until she was weak from laughter.

In moments like this, it all seemed possible to her. She really would marry him and he would sing the right kind of songs—they would always be children in love.

But you belong to Christ, the persistent voice whispered. *First, most importantly, you belong to the Father through Christ*.

"I want to love you," she said out loud. Joe's mouth was only inches from her own. "I want to know that we're supposed to be husband and wife together—that we've a blessing on us."

"Of course," he murmured, his long-lashed eyes closed, "of course we have a blessing. Don't you know that?" And he kissed her again, sweetly, deeply.

And somewhere in the middle of that kiss, Morning realized that if she wanted Joe, wanted the changes in him, she was going to have to put up a terrible fight!

"I wish you wouldn't do that," Joe said from the doorway of the kitchen.

Morning, who was busily making golden, fluffy omelets, filled with Monterey mushrooms, turned from the big stove. She had been up over an hour. Very early she'd risen, showered, washed her hair, and put on a simple, pale green cotton dress, chic enough for Carmel but simple enough to wash and wear while traveling. She had coiled her sun-lit brown hair on top of her head and stuck in a few tiny white violets she'd found growing just outside Joe's kitchen door.

"Wish I wouldn't do what? Joe, please don't step on that part of the kitchen floor. I just scrubbed it and it isn't dry over there."

He stared at her. "You just scrubbed the floor? Hey, I pay people a lot of money to do stuff like that!" He looked around. "Where's Mrs. Monahan?"

"Stella? I gave her the day off. It's Sunday, Joe. She said she wanted to go to church and I told her just to take the day." She poured the omelet mixture into the skillet. "I hope you don't mind."

He came over to her, barefooted, wearing faded jeans and no shirt. His broad, tanned chest still glistened with water from his shower. He stood behind Morning as she cooked and, very gently, began to kiss the nape of her neck.

"Joe, please...I can't—" she turned around and as

98

she did, he pulled her close and playfully kissed her mouth.

"You're going to make the omelets burn," she said somewhat breathlessly.

"But you taste so much better than breakfast! Mmm…come here, honey—"

Morning gently eased out of his grasp. "I haven't got too much time, Joe. Church starts at nine-thirty and I want to be there in plenty of time."

He looked surprised. "Church?"

"I found the newspaper at your front door, and I turned to the religious section and found a church nearby in Pacific Grove that we can go to." She went over and opened the cupboard doors, looking for plates. "We can bring back groceries for dinner," she told him. "Your guests last night seem to have eaten everything you'd stocked in."

"Church," Joe said, his voice low. He went over and sat at the small table near the sliding glass door. "Look, Morning, I've got some phone calls to make and some business to take care of. You go on and when you get back, we can have a swim and then have the rest of the day to ourselves. And I don't want you to cook. We'll have dinner someplace on the Wharf tonight. Okay?"

Not okay, but she could only nod and smile brightly. *Well, you didn't really expect him to jump at the idea of going with you to church, did you?*

It was a picturesque, lovely little church in Pacific Grove, a village just on the other side of the town of Monterey. Morning sat quietly listening to the minister talk of the great miracles of Jesus, and afterwards, people began to walk forward, each in turn giving witness to a miracle in their own lives. One young man told of his joy in his new freedom from drugs and alcohol. A woman holding her baby told of God's hand on her and her child in a nearly fatal automobile accident several months before. All of these people were deeply grateful to the Lord for what had been done for them.

Leaving the church after shaking hands with several people sitting near her, Morning felt more certain than ever that marriage to Joe Hunter was impossible. She had meant to go to church, sing, listen, and kneel in prayer—prayer for Joe and herself. She had done that. She had prayed for Joe, asking God to touch him, to open his eyes and ears.

But surprisingly, her deepest prayer had been for her dad.

She had sat in that unfamiliar yet love-filled church and remembered her dad—not as he was now but as he had once been—laughing and merry and charming and strong. And even though it was supposed to be hopeless, even though the doctors had told them it was indeed hopeless—still, she had prayed for a miracle. *Father in heaven, help my dad. Help my dad—remember, he belongs to You. Sick as he is, he still belongs to You!*

She made up her mind that when this trip to Chicago and this week with Joe were finished, she would return home to see her parents.

Chapter Seven

Joe was on the front deck, sitting in front of a table. He was playing his guitar, writing on a sheet of paper, drinking coffee, and watching the road for her. He waved as she drove up in his easy-to-drive antique car and met her halfway up the steps.

"Hi. My mother always wanted me to marry a girl who wears apple green and goes to church and smells like—mmm—lilac. Come on. I've got a surprise for you."

"Joe, I want to talk to you."

He glanced at her, seeing that her eyes were serious. "Later. Right now, I want to introduce you to someone."

She didn't really feel up to company, but she dutifully followed him through the house to the kitchen. Nobody there. Then she saw the half-grown puppy trundle out of a box in the corner.

"His name is Rags," Joe told her. "Named after the first dog I ever had. My dad found him in the swamp and brought him home. This guy showed up while I was on the beach this morning."

The young dog's tail beat wildly against Joe's legs.

He licked Joe's hands and face and growled at Morning.

"Joe, he's soaking wet!"

"I rubbed him down when I pulled him out of the sea. But his coat hasn't dried out completely yet."

"I thought you said you found him on the beach."

"Well—sort of the beach. Not too far out." He looked at her. "Okay, so I saw him out there and I swam out and got him."

So that was why he and the puppy both looked exhausted. Morning knelt and coaxed the little dog into trusting her.

"You could have told me the truth, you know," she said. "I wouldn't get mad at you because you risked your life to save a puppy that somebody probably threw off a boat."

"It doesn't matter," he told her gruffly. "Neither of us drowned."

As usual, he didn't want to talk about something he had done that a lot of people might have called foolish. But a lot of people, including Morning, knew he couldn't seem to help himself. If someone was old or sick or broke or drowning, Joe Hunter could no more turn away than he could stop writing his songs.

They had lunch on the front deck. By that time Rags felt totally at home, to the point of barking when the housekeeper came by with freshly made chess pies. As they were savoring their last bites, Joe began to talk to Morning about his music.

"After you left for church," he told her, "I had this …this feeling…about you, about us—and it kind of took over. Words and sounds began to filter into me and I started at the piano and then switched to the guitar because that way I could work on it out here and watch for you."

"When do I get to hear it?"

"When it's finished. Maybe when we get back from Chicago." He looked at her. "It's called 'One Last Goodby.' It's sort of about a guy who keeps on coming back to his woman, even though she always ends it. Even though he knows it'll happen—that she'll leave him, he keeps on coming back."

Their eyes met in silent knowing. To talk of getting married, they both knew, was just a part of the fantasy-dream. It wouldn't, couldn't happen. They both knew she was going to leave him again. And, Morning realized, she really didn't have to talk to Joe about it, because he already knew what the reason was.

"I think," Morning said finally, "I'll borrow your car and go to the supermarket over off the Valley Road. I just brought home enough food for lunch. You go right on working and I'll be back very soon."

He nodded. The moment had passed, the moment when the truth came to them both: he didn't really want to change his life. He wanted her, but he wanted his lifestyle too—or at least, some parts of it.

Morning was more or less expecting the call from Reneé that afternoon. The phone rang as she was trying on the new swimsuit she'd bought on her way to the grocery. She'd gone to a big discount place in Salinas, where mostly working-class people shopped. Seeing the mothers with children and babies in the big carts, older ladies wandering around looking at sheets and towels on sale, husbands driving up in front to help load the car with the sacks of whatever—somehow made her feel better. It might seem, at times, that there were no people in the world but those like Toby, but there were other kinds of people too, working people who married and shopped for diapers and sheets and towels on sale.

She'd just pulled on the pretty, yellow, one-piece suit—modest and yet very becoming to her slender figure—when Joe called up the stairs to her.

"Honey? Hey! Dragon Lady wants you on the phone."

She very nearly asked him to say she wasn't there, which she wouldn't be, if she hurried out the glass door to the beach for a swim. But she didn't. After all, Renée's firm paid her salary and she did have a responsibility to them.

"Okay," she said, and she realized that Joe was looking at her. He smiled, pleased, and offered her a glass of iced tea. Morning's face flushed. She'd meant to put on Joe's robe but it wasn't anyplace around. Still, she was again thankful that her body was slender and, although not gorgeous, nice enough.

"I really ought to fire you, you know," Renée told her icily. "Why didn't you let me know you were going back to Carmel?"

"I was going to let you know, Renée. All in good time." Morning winked at Joe, who sat not so far from her, still softly strumming chords on the guitar and making copious notes.

"I had a call from Marcella Stratton," Renée said, still in that same displeased tone. "She isn't sure if she's going ahead with plans for her house, the one she was going to spend all that money on."

"Well, I'm really not too surprised," Morning said. "She said she was going to Mexico to think, and she probably decided—"

"I don't think you quite understand, darling. It's entirely up to you to get that account back. Frankly, the firm can't stand losing a big one like that. It'll look ex-

104

tremely bad for both of us."

"But I can't, Renée," Morning said carefully, "If Marcella changed her mind about redecorating that house, I'm sure she has a very good reason."

"Reasons don't matter," Renée told her crisply. "The point is, you've got to get her to decide to go ahead with the work. Tell her anything you like."

"Renée, she might have changed her mind about marrying that man."

"Who, her? Darling, she adores getting married! She does it all the time, every other year or so. So forget that idea."

"Renée, I mean it. I think she might be going through some very deep changes and—"

"You're wasting our time," Renée told her. "I want you to get a call in to Marcella right away and see what you can do. And I don't want you to botch up the Hunter account. Are you firm on that?"

"Yes, of course." She smiled at Joe. "Mr. Hunter wants me to do his house with the garden theme."

Joe got up and came over to her, nuzzling her ear warmly, teasing her. "Make that the Garden of Eden," he whispered.

"Morning, are you still there?"

"Yes—yes. I just said things are—fine here."

"No truth to that silly rumor that you're going to marry him, is there? There was an item on one of those silly television shows where they gossip about people—"

"No," Morning said quickly. "That's not so, Renée."

"I didn't think so. I told you before, darling, I never thought of you as being a great beauty, and I'm sure he can have girls who are."

"Yes. That's right, Renée." She moved gently away from Joe, who was trying to go on kissing her neck.

"Renée, I'll be in touch later. I've mailed the cost sheet to you and the work can start here within the week, after they get the damp air problem taken care of and get some ceilings washed. Bye for now."

"What isn't so?" Joe asked, going back to his guitar.

She decided to avoid his question. If she told him the newspapers probably had the "item" about them as well as the network television stations, she would have to come right out and admit that she wasn't going to marry him. He already knew that, and he knew why, but talking about it would only spoil the time they had left.

They took a charter flight from Monterey to San Francisco, where Joe was instantly recognized. As they hurried through the terminal to catch the departing flight to Chicago, a small crowd of girls and women followed him, laughing, teasing, flirting, hanging on to him. Morning, beside him, carrying her small traveling case and handbag, watched in near horror as a woman grabbed the suitcase Joe was carrying, opened it, and stole the shirt he was to wear for that night's concert.

On the plane, they were silent until the stewardess brought the dinner menus.

"I'll just have the salad, please," Morning said, "and tea."

Having ordered a steak, Joe leaned back and turned his head to look at her.

"Morning," he said, his voice low, "I'm sorry."

"It couldn't be helped. I hope you've got another one of those fancy shirts, though." She tried to keep her voice light.

He put his hand over hers. "Toby was supposed to clear the way. He was supposed to arrange for us to transfer to this flight in a car that was going to drive us on the runway to the plane." His voice was edged with anger. "I'll have to have a talk with him in Chicago."

Morning said nothing, but as she ate the slightly wilted salad and sipped the weak tea, she wondered if perhaps Toby—Connard, his last name was—might not have deliberately failed to arrange for that private car in San Francisco just so those women would spot Joe. He surely knew how she hated the pawing, the grabbing, the open displays of sexuality from those girls and women. He must have seen that on her face at Joe's unexpected party, when the young woman danced suggestively and stared at Joe the whole time.

Toby had promised her he'd get rid of her if he had to, and he just might be proving his point. She felt upset, angry and tired and uneasy when the women behaved that way around him. It seemed appalling to her, the frantic arms, hands, reaching out to touch him, the feverish faces, the bright look of desire in their eyes—

I know what it is, she thought suddenly. *They worship him! Those women worship him—and that's why it's so terribly wrong!*

There was a limo waiting at O'Hare Airport for them. Toby sat back, smiling his somewhat oily smile, behaving as if he were delighted to see Morning.

"Big press party in forty-five minutes, Joe-baby. I fixed things so it will be in a party room at the hotel. That way you two can have your little private time before the concert." He gazed out the window. Morning felt certain he knew full well that his insinuation angered both her and Joe.

"I'm not in the mood for a press party," Joe said evenly. He leaned forward in the plush seat. "Would you mind telling me, ole buddy, why there wasn't a car waiting in San Francisco to take us to the plane? Did

107

you get so busy counting money that you forgot to set it up?"

"Hey," Toby said smoothly, "Joe-baby, I tried! It isn't easy to get permission to do that! I know there hasn't been a problem in the past, but San Francisco International security is tough, baby, real tough."

"I think, Toby-baby," Joe said quietly, "you're lying in your teeth. We'll talk later, when my lady isn't here."

Morning was silent next to Joe. She was beginning to wonder if she should have come. Somebody—one of those wild women who'd followed him through the airport—would call the papers, and before very long, another item would appear—*Joe Hunter and Latest go to Newtown concert in Chi*—something like that. Reneé would see it, and get on the phone at once, most likely. Reneé still maintained "that sort of thing" was not at all good for the firm's spotless reputation. And she was quite right about that.

Nobody, certainly not Reneé, would believe she and Joe weren't sleeping together.

And neither, she thought, her hands trembling slightly at the thought, *would her mother.*

Joe refused to attend the press party, which provoked a barrage of phone calls, some of them to Morning's room on a separate floor from Joe's. The hotel was very old, famous and elegant. Joe had a suite of some sort and she had a lovely penthouse apartment with sitting room and dressing room. Joe had surely had one of his people phone and make sure her room was lovely.

As the sky darkened, Chicago's lights came on and the penthouse view was stunning. There was, she realized, a certain feeling about Chicago, maybe from the look of the people, especially the men. The young man who'd carried their bags for them had a slight brogue. And the men seemed huskier than men in San Francisco. Chicago, *City of the Big Shoulders*, its poet had sung.

She liked it, always had.

In Joe's suite, early dinner was brought for them on a cart. Morning had bathed, enjoyed a cup of delicious coffee in her room, and now, in her white pantsuit and bright blue silk blouse, she sat comfortably near the huge glassed-in wall of his living room.

"You look beautiful," he told her. "If I had to guess, I'd say you were a California girl. The tan tells all." He buttered a warm roll for her as if she were a delightful child.

"Well, I'm not," Morning said. "I'm not a California girl. And for my money, Chicago is a lovely, lovely town."

"Wait," he said, "until you get a load of Nashville. Now there's a really great town." He was watching her. "I've got some old snapshots of my parents' wedding day, in front of the church in Nashville where they got married. I'll show them to you when we get back to Carmel."

She felt her face color, and she had to avoid his eyes.

"Yes," she said, cutting the tender fish, "I'd like to see that."

"Morning, even if it can't happen, I meant what I said about wanting to marry you."

"Joe, don't—please—not now." She finally made herself meet his steady blue gaze. "Let's not spoil things," she said softly.

He caught her hand and kissed the palm. "I know what you want," he told her. "I know the kind of man you want me to be. That's what makes it so tough. I just don't think I can live up to that."

"Joe—darling, you don't understand!" Her voice

was earnest. She hadn't realized he'd think that of her, that she only wanted him to have a certain kind of image, behave in a certain way.

"All I want," she told him, "all I've ever wanted was for us both to belong to Christ and to make our lives a kind of lovely tribute to His love. Joe, through your music, you could change so many lives, turn people around, put them right in the arms of God. If only you'd—"

"Hey," he said, obviously very uncomfortable, "honey, I'm a composer, a singer—not a missionary!" Suddenly he got up from the table. "I've got to dress for the gig. Call room service if you want anything else."

She nodded. She didn't want anything else. She'd lost her appetite. He didn't understand, not at all. He didn't know how easy it would be to call on the name of the Lord for help. He thought it had to do with showing up at church and suddenly becoming somehow more to her liking. He just didn't understand, because he really didn't want to.

The subject of marriage almost came up again in the limo, as they drove from the back alley behind the hotel across town to the section known as Newtown.

"I've been thinking," he said in the near-darkness, "about us."

She had her head on his shoulder. He looked wonderful, his face was tanned and freshly shaven, his dark hair still glistened from the shower, and he wore the low-cut white shirt with flowing sleeves that had become his trademark on stage. Oh, the women would love him tonight, up there on that stage!

"This isn't," she told him, "a very good time to do that. Seems to me you ought to be concentrating on the show."

110

"Not interested." He looked down at her. "Well, maybe this gig does interest me a little, because I'm going to do all the songs I like best."

"No leather and electronic lights?"

"I've sent down word," he told her. "Tonight it's going to be what I think they're calling 'a love experience.' It's going to be laid-back and easy, nice and easy. If the guys working the lights haven't got word, I'll stop the show and ask them to do it the way I want it."

"Joe, would you really—"

But he would. She knew he would. And his fans would eat that up—Joe up there giving orders.

She braced herself for the women who would probably be waiting at the theatre to mob him.

As soon as the limo pulled up in front of the stage door, it began. Morning had been right. There must have been over a hundred women standing there, all of them trying to touch him as he hurried through the crowd to the stage door. Some of his people were there to try to keep the girls back, but it must have been an impossible task—one of the girls screamed and managed to throw something at him. It glanced off his left cheek just under his eye. A thin trickle of blood showed.

Morning felt half sick as she was pushed, shoved both by the women and Joe's body guards, toward the darkened stage door. Just before she was pushed safely inside, she half turned and saw the woman, about twenty-five, quite good looking, but wild-eyed, try to throw the object at him again.

It was a key. Probably a room key.

Morning was shown to what they called the "green room," a waiting and gathering room for the show people. A few people from Joe's back-up band were there briefly, having coffee and talking. They glanced

Morning and nodded politely, but it was quite clear that they didn't like having a stranger along when they played a show with Joe. Or maybe, she thought, it wasn't that at all. Maybe it had to do with the fact that Joe wasn't going to go wild tonight, as the tabloids called it.

The musicians left, and she could hear them tuning up on-stage. She'd given Joe a quick kiss in his dressing room and now she was alone in this pleasant room with the coffee bar and sandwiches. No, not alone. Toby had just walked in. "Enjoying yourself so far? How do you like Chicago?" he asked.

He wants something, she thought. *He's come in here to try to get me to change my mind about something.*

"Yes," she told him uneasily, "I've always liked Chicago."

He smiled at her, but his eyes stayed cold behind the tinted glasses. "I keep forgetting—you come from these parts, right?"

"Wrong. I come from the Midwest, but not Chicago." *Go away*, she thought, *go away. You frighten me!*

"And the first time you stayed at Joe's house…let's see…wasn't that about five years ago? The first time you guys made it together—you must have been just a young kid!"

Her heart seemed to have stopped. "How—who told you I knew Joe before?"

He helped himself to coffee. "Just somebody who was around at that time and who's still around. One of Joe's people. He remembered that time in Malibu— said he remembered your face, even though you were much more of a kid then and now you've filled out considerably." He smiled at her again, pouring sugar

112

into the coffee. "You know something, honey? It would make a great story if the press knew you'd been sort of his—child lover—and now you're back on what we might call a grand scale. '*Baby-doll lover turns into sexy woman. He loved her then—he loves her lots more now!*'"

She stared at him. "Are—are you saying you're going to turn that kind of—filth—about Joe and me—over to the tabloids?"

"Sweetie, did I say that? Hey—I work for Joe, remember!"

"I could tell him," she said, her voice husky with feeling. "If you dare to let them print that filth, I swear I'll tell Joe it was you who phoned it in!"

"Not me, honey. Maybe one of his people, but not me." He put down the coffee cup. "Tonight's show might be a kind of change for his fans. They'll go for it tonight okay—no problem."

"If you'll excuse me," she said, "Joe wants me backstage before the curtain goes up."

He blocked her way again. "This time he can get by with all the sad, sweet numbers. It's a packed house and this town is more apt to go for those love songs. But when it comes to L.A. and Frisco, he's got to get back to the bad, mad, mean stuff. If he doesn't, he could start slipping. And with this movie deal pending, I'm not going to let that happen."

She looked at him levelly. "I told you before—as long as I have any influence on Joe, he isn't going to dish out that kind of electronic garbage to those people!"

His eyes didn't change, except for two small pin points of light, like tiny candles, burning deep in them. Morning realized with a shock that this man hated her, truly hated her.

Well, hadn't Jesus promised that if you belonged to Him, the world would hate you?

Joe had a three-legged, high stool on stage as a prop, but he didn't sit on it as he sang. Instead, he held the mike in one hand and walked back and forth, down-stage, close to the audience. His voice was low, throb-bing with feeling as he sang "Shadow Dance," then, "Was It Rain or Was It Tears." Both brought down the house with screams and cheers. He followed with newer songs, "Me and My Baby," then the newest one, "One Last Goodby," which the band had only run through a few times earlier that evening. He went into some of his lighter songs, easing again into the more dramatic "She's Gone," "Summer's End," and finally—beautifully rendered—"Morning's Song."

The audience, men and women alike, wanted more. They all stood up, yelling, clapping, whistling, scream-ing. Somebody started chanting Joe's name and others picked it up, until the rafters fairly shook with the loud, insistent voices.

He did one more number for them, one that had brought him a gold record—"Let Me Come Back One More Time."

Watching from her position backstage, standing near several lighting technicians who worked on a big switchboard, Morning felt tears come to her eyes. Yes, Joe could get his audiences to do just about whatever he wanted. He could make them feel love as they felt tonight, or hate, as they must have felt at some of his other concerts, when he was performing the way Toby wanted him to.

He looked for her as soon as he came off-stage with the screaming and the applause following him. His "people" thronged around him at once. One of them handed him a towel to wipe his face, one of them offered him a big glass of water, and several of them were talking about the show, patting him on the back. The drummer from the band wanted to ask him about the new number, and the girls who sang back-up complained to him about not having gotten copies of the words soon enough.

Somehow, through the crowd, he pulled her along beside him, firmly holding onto her hand. Morning tried to be pleasant and unobtrusive, but it was very hard, right there in the center of all that talk and movement.

Finally, in his dressing room, there were only herself, Joe, and Toby, who was smiling and behaving as if he really liked her.

"Great, Joe-baby. Just great! They love you when you're in love," Toby said, making it sound as if Joe was in love with someone else every other month or so. "We'll play this theme out here in the Midwest, and slowly get a little sexier, as we get to—"

"I told you," Joe said, changing shirts, putting on a jacket, and getting ready to leave, "I don't want to do an electronic show." He glanced at Morning. "Toby, go on out and clear the way. Tell those people I've left by a side door or something. This time, when my girl and I walk out there, I don't want anybody to be there, except my own people. Got that?" His voice was level. "I don't like it when Morning gets pushed around out there. So make sure it doesn't happen." Joe's usual light, easy manner was gone. His eyes were angry. "Because," he went on, "I'm getting these little messages in my brain, telling me that all these mess-ups aren't just accidents, that you're letting people come around, letting them wait for me, on purpose."

"Joe—hey—why would I—"

"Just make sure it's all clear," Joe told him.

It was. This time it was. She and Joe walked through a hallway to a door. A young man nodded and held it open, and parked just outside was a limousine with its lights off.

Joe helped her in and got in beside her. Someone slammed the door shut. There was a glass partition. Joe leaned forward, slid it open and said simply, "Let's get out of here." Immediately, the car's lights went on and it shot forward.

They were driving through the city, through that downtown section known as the Loop. Again, Joe leaned forward and slid back the glass that separated them from the driver.

"Is there a deli around here?"

The driver began talking about where one could get the best sandwiches. Joe listened politely. Finally something was settled, and again he closed the glass and sat beside Morning.

"I hope you like barbeque," he said.

"Love it." She gazed out the window at the lights of the city, feeling somehow quite content for the moment, here in this big, fast car, sitting next to Joe, knowing he needed her—for a while, at least. She found it hard to believe that his intense feeling would last—that their fantasy time would, if they wanted it to, go on and on. Too many problems. Too many women in love with him, wanting to take him to their beds.

"Take a right after we get the food," Joe told the driver some ten minutes later, as they again pulled up on a dark side street.

The big sack of food smelled wonderful. The driver made a right turn at the next light and very soon they were driving along Lake Shore Drive. They continued

116

on, until the downtown lights were behind them. This part of the beach looked nearly deserted.

"Okay," Joe said suddenly, leaning forward. He tapped on the glass and the big car pulled to the curb.

"Joe," Morning said, "what—"

"Come on, honey," he told her. "Bring the food."

"But we aren't getting out here, are we?"

He had gotten out and now came around to open the door for her himself.

"It's safe enough," he told her. "Besides, Bobby there in the car gets paid to help me out in case I get jumped."

"I'm not sure you and your bodyguard could do much in this dark," she told him. It was very dark indeed, but there was a cool breeze coming off the lake and there was sand under their feet. But even the smell of the lake and the still-warm sand didn't change the fact that this was Chicago, a big, tough, mean, and even dangerous city. In Carmel, people walked the beach at night all the time. Here it seemed ill-advised.

"Don't be scared," Joe told her, putting a protective arm around her. "I've got a black belt, so relax."

Karate. Yes, she had read somewhere that he had that, that he could take care of himself with or without his paid bodyguards, like Bobby, who had left the car and stood on the beach not too far from them, smoking.

Joe had her sit on the sand while he opened the big sack containing their food. First, he took the paper napkins and spread them on the sand. Then he put out the sandwiches and big cups of coffee in paper cups and the slaw and the still-hot potato balls, a speciality of the house, Bobby had told them.

"Hey, Bob—go get a steak or something and come back for us."

117

The dark figure turned in surprise. "But—"

"We'll be fine. Just come back in half an hour or so."

And so the big limo drove off and they were alone on the dark beach. They sat huddled close, eating the delicious food. He wanted to feed her the potatoes one by one, putting each one into her mouth and then kissing her when her mouth was full of potato. He was, she saw, having a great time.

"I'll do the rest of the tour later," he told her. "When we leave Chicago tomorrow, we'll have plenty of time to relax back in Carmel. Oh—by the way, are you happy with that crazy little dump you live in on Telegraph Hill?"

"I suppose so," she told him. "I like living in a neighborhood, even if nobody ever says good morning to me. It's part of the fantasy of California, I guess."

"I'm going to buy that house for you," he said off-handedly. "Pass the mustard, honey."

"You—you're going to *what*?"

"I like that house," he told her. "I like thinking about you there, in that kitchen, or on that porch in the back, where you can sit down and look at the city. Unless, of course, you'd rather I bought you a condo someplace else."

"I can't let you do that," she said quietly, beginning to feel unreasonably annoyed and not sure why. "I don't want you doing that sort of thing for me. Buying me a house. I mean it, Joe. I don't want that."

"Look, I buy stuff for people all the time! I like to give people presents. It's one of my selfish habits," he told her lightly. "That way, they can't ever get rid of me. I can come to your house in the middle of the night and ask you to fix me bacon and eggs, and you'll do it. I mean, you'll think of me as a nice guy, and you'll let me in, out of the rain."

"Do you always do this, Joe?"

He kissed her gently. "Mmmm. Do what? Buy houses for ladies?"

"Yes. Do you?"

"Never. Never have. Never knew a girl I'd want to make feel she had to get up and cook for me." He kissed her again, his eyes were closed. "How come you always taste so good?"

"Don't—please don't buy that house, Joe. I don't want it. I really don't."

"I'm very determined," he said, mouth against hers, "to keep you in my world, in case you haven't noticed. And all this talk about one week is a lot of hogwash."

She moved her face to one side. He could make her heart beat so loud, so hard, when he kissed her this way, she was sure he must be able to hear it pounding.

"Just promise me you won't buy that house for me."

"Okay. I'll buy you one in Nashville, then. I told you," he said, "it's the most beautiful city in the world. Better than Carmel, better than San Francisco or Chicago—" he was looking at her. "What's wrong, Morning? What's the matter?"

"I—I've decided I want to go home."

"What? You mean back to San Francisco? What about the rest of our time together? I thought we promised each other we'd have this one, beautiful week!" He moved away from her, clearly getting angry. "Of course, I admit I wasn't really being honest with you. I mean, I wasn't going to let you walk away from me at the end of the week."

"And buying me a house just might help me change my mind?"

He let his breath out. "Okay. So I bribe people. Is that what you mean?"

She put a gentle hand on his arm. "Joe, I'm not talking about San Francisco or that little house I rent. I'm talking about home—where my parents are," she said quietly.

"You're saying you want to bust up our time together so you can visit your parents?" He suddenly lay back on the sand, putting his hands behind his head, staring up at the starry black sky over Chicago. "Seems to me I've heard that before. Little girl feels the guy is getting too close to taking her to bed, so she leaves, runs home to—"

"Joe, that isn't fair! When I—when I left you in Malibu five years ago, it was because my mother called me to tell me Daddy had a stroke, that he might be dying!"

There was a silence. "Okay," he said finally, turning his head to look at her. "I'm sorry. That was uncalled for, and I apologize."

"Maybe," she said, "we'd better go."

"Morning, I said I'm sorry!"

"I just don't think you understand," she told him, beginning to put the empty cups in the sack. Crumpling up the napkins, she put them in there too. "You're so used to having people come and go at your beck and call—"

And as if proof were suddenly presented, the big limo pulled up at the curb and cut its lights, waiting discreetly for them.

"If you want to get me out of your life," he told her, "just tell me, okay? Look, we haven't talked about that guy in your life. I didn't want to ask questions and I figured maybe you'd decided he didn't really matter. But when you tell me you can't even give me one week with you, that you have to find some excuse and run back, I'd be a fool to think he doesn't have something to do with it!"

"There isn't any other man, Joe," she said quietly.

"Sure."

"I mean it. There never was. Over the years, I've dated, yes, but I haven't—there wasn't anyone else I wanted, I guess." She gently put her hands on his face. It felt hot from his sudden anger. "I wanted to talk to you about giving your life to Christ," she said softly. "But you didn't—I guess I didn't think I could convince you of anything. I still feel that way, Joe. So I just let you think there was another man in my life. I'm sorry."

"I guess," he said, his face close to hers, his blue eyes not so angry now, "I ought to feel better now. But I don't."

"I had this idea," she told him, "that together, we could sit on the deck at your house in Carmel and that we could study together. Study the Bible. And that you'd want to know more and more. And that as you grew in knowledge, you'd want to—"

"Fire all the people who work for me? Tell them I've suddenly become Holy Joe Hunter and I'm not gonna sing anymore or play my music?"

"Joe, I didn't mean—"

"Why can't you just relax and let us be happy, Morning? It's a miracle that we found each other again, and you're trying to spoil our second time around by changing me into—"

"It wasn't," she told him, "a miracle. At least—not the sort that just suddenly happens when you least expect it."

"What?"

"I tried to get that assignment for weeks," she said. "The truth is, Joe, I wanted to see you again. Nobody pushed this job at me and said I had to do it or get fired. It wasn't that way at all. I wanted very much to

121

see you again. I suppose," she said softly, "I wanted to get you out of my system."

"And have you?"

She went to him, leaning against him, holding him.

"You know I haven't! Surely you must know I—how I feel about you—"

"Tell me, then," he said, drawing her even closer to himself. "Tell me, sweetheart—"

She closed her eyes against the bright, watching stars.

"I love you, Joe. I love you!"

He kissed her. The kiss was deep and urgent. Morning responded by kissing him back, hugging him, letting her love for him flow like wine. But then: "Joe—please—please—no!"

"I need you," he whispered. "Don't you understand how much I need you? You're my light, Morning, in a world that gets to be too much—"

"Joe—please—don't—" and she moved away from him, glancing over at the big car parked in the near-darkness.

"Yeah. I forgot about Bobby. Okay, let's go back to the hotel." He suddenly looked at her. "You know I won't—touch you, ever—not if you don't want me to."

But on the ride back to the hotel, there was a strained silence. His hand covered hers, but even that didn't seem to bring them closer. Hadn't she known this time would come, when he would want her to give her body to him and she would refuse? He could promise all he wanted, but he must be hurting at her rejection—just as his attitude about her wanting him to be "Holy Joe" hurt her.

They said good night in the silent hallway outside her suite on the penthouse floor. His eyes told her he was still hurt and angry and that he wanted to be asked to come inside her room. But she kissed his cheek briefly, let him unlock the door and then she was inside, saying good night again, closing the door between them.

She stood with her back to the door for a few seconds, trying to put down her impulse to open it, run after him, bring him back here with her so they could be together.

It was very late, only hours from dawn. She would say goodby to him here in Chicago, she decided. She was only forty-five minutes away from her parents' home, by jet flight. There was no need to go all the way back to Carmel with Joe and leave from there. The house, his house, was ready as far as her part went. She had ordered the crews, set up time schedules, gotten prices okayed, and gone over colors and fabric and wallpaper with Joe, who usually didn't seem very interested, but left most of it up to her.

There was still Marcella Stratton's house in L.A. to worry about. Renée had ordered her to get Marcella to go ahead with her plans to redecorate.

Well, she wasn't going to do that. Renée could fire her over this—and she very well might. But right now, Los Angeles was the last place on earth she wanted to be.

She showered, put on her nightgown, and crawled wearily into bed. Living Joe's hectic schedule wasn't easy. She lay there in bed, worn out from the busy day and night, but still not able to sleep. Joe wanted them to go on together. He wanted to buy her things, keep her in his life.

He was even willing to marry her. But he wouldn't, she knew, change for her. And the worst part was, he didn't even know what she meant when she talked

123

about his giving his life to Christ.

Sometime before she drifted into a light, fitful sleep, she decided that since Joe loved giving gifts, she would give him a gift too—a Bible. She would buy it before they left Chicago.

She woke to the gentle tapping on her door. It was probably a breakfast tray. Morning put on her robe, pushed her hair back from her face and went to open it. It was a grey, rainy day in Chicago. Outside the window of that room, the city seemed to hunch down under the cold downpour. There had been thunder earlier, and lightning streaking across the sky as she tried to get to sleep. Funny, she didn't ever remember hearing thunder in California. She'd somehow missed that. Thunderstorms had been a sound she'd grown up with.

And there was her breakfast, on one of those little carts, with a smiling bellboy bringing it in.

"Mr. Hunter wants you to have the schedule for the day," he told her, handing her a piece of paper. "He wants you to know he's got a business meeting until noon, and the plane leaves at two. He'd like you to join him for lunch."

"Thank you," Morning said tiredly.

So he had sent her a message. He hadn't bothered to ring her room and invite her to lunch himself. *Did he,* she wondered as she sipped the strong coffee, leaving the hot food untouched, *think that she ought to be so thrilled, delighted and honored to be here with him that she ought to just sit around and wait for time to join him? "Here are your orders for the day, Miss Edford. See that you keep your appointment."*

Well, perhaps she was being foolish. Fatigue, a genuine pressing need to see her parents, and a kind of guilt

124

over what she was doing to her job had made her careless in her thinking.

Joe loves me and he doesn't mean to hurt me. No. Joe thinks he loves me but his work comes first and foremost!

The latter was, she knew, far closer to the truth.

She showered and dressed after a second cup of coffee and a few moments to open her Bible, which she always took with her, even though she had, over the years, stopped daily readings.

She opened it at random, saw she had come upon Song of Solomon, and the words glared at her, touching her mind and heart: "I am my beloved's, and my beloved is mine."

She bowed her head, there at that fragile writing desk set next to the window. *All right, Lord. I'll accept, then, that Joe loves me. That he isn't just riding some fantasy because we were once young and in love.*

But loving her and wanting to make love to her weren't enough.

Chapter Eight

There was something comforting about walking in the Chicago rain alone, under a huge black umbrella she had just bought at Carson's. Back in San Francisco, there was a very small web of certain people, of a certain age and income and lifestyle, who were always running into each other at fashionable cafés, the theatre, the ballet at the Opera House. Bright and upcoming, they were called. Intent on making a lot of money, all of them.

And she'd been no better. She had thrown herself into what had seemed like not only a dream job in a very exciting city, but also a chance to escape from the horror of what had happened to her father. *Maybe*, she thought, striding along through the morning crowd, *I was running out on Mother*. And yet, that didn't really seem possible, since her mother obviously had found a new life for herself and seemed very happy about it.

Before her mother remarried—and she'd no idea when or how soon that might be—she wanted to return home and see her parents, or at least see them one at a time and remember the family as it had once been.

In the meantime, she was enjoying her anonymity

here. A taxi drove up and splashed dirty water up to her waist. Morning very nearly stuck her tongue out at the driver, but she didn't and, not really wanting to turn the other cheek, she sloshed on. She finally found a tiny bookstore that smelled of dust and leather binding, and there she chose a Bible for Joe. The cover was sturdy and it was the right size for traveling.

She walked along the wide street by the grey lake and she thought about other places to live. When she left, resumed her life, she need not be one of Renée's ambitious little decorators. It need not be in California at all. Perhaps, she told herself, she ought to live in a place like Chicago—grim, tough, sturdy. When she left, perhaps she ought to consider…

When she left?

When I leave Joe.

Morning walked through the lobby with her head high, hoping nobody would hear the strange sound her soaked shoes made whenever she took a step. On the elevator up to the penthouse, she kept her eyes modestly on the climbing arrow. Two people who shared the same kind of accommodation down the hall from her also shared the ride. The man, middle-aged and jolly, gave her a look of good-natured approval, but the woman stared at her feet, under which was a small puddle from her soaked clothes.

Still, she felt strong as she let herself into her suite. She switched on lights, for the day was still dark, and as she headed for the bathroom she saw Joe sitting in a chair, halfway facing the window and halfway facing the door.

"I guess I can call the police now," he said, "and tell them to stop looking for you."

"Joe—you didn't!" She looked hastily at her watch.

Yes, she was nearly an hour late for their luncheon date. "I'm sorry," she said. "Please—tell me you didn't really call the police."

"Okay, I didn't really call the police. Any young lady who makes it on her own in L.A. is probably safe in Chicago." He came closer to her. "What'd you do—fall in the lake?"

"No. I—I walked," she told him. "Joe, I've got to get out of these clothes and take a shower."

"As soon as we get home to Carmel," he yelled after her, "I'm sticking you in the hot tub! Understand?" He was following her down the hallway.

"Joe," she said, "I'm not going back to Carmel just now. I've got to see my parents, my mother and dad. I need to see them. I can't explain it. But please try to understand."

"Why now? Why during this week you promised we'd have? Look—I busted up my road schedule, lied to the press about missing concerts, got the guys in the band mad at me for breaking a contract, got my lawyers on my neck, had to put up with some crooked doctor who said he'd give me a medical certificate saying I'm too tired or something to make the gigs on time—and all of a sudden, after all that garbage I went through to be with you—you tell me you want to cut out and go home to your parents!"

"Joe," she said shakily, hating to see anger in his eyes this way, "I'm going to take a shower." And she shut the door behind her firmly.

But even after she'd turned on the shower, hot and steamy, got out of her clothes, and put on the shower cap she'd found pinned to the curtain, his voice came to her, still angry:

"When are you gonna grow up, little girl? When are you gonna start thinking like a woman? When—"

She turned up the shower, so she couldn't hear.

Was she, then, afraid of physical love with him? Was that a part of this urge to leave, to return to the place where she'd been so happy as a child?

When she stepped out of the shower, all was silent. She wrapped herself in the big towel provided and opened the door.

"Joe?"

No answer. She crept down the hallway, clutching the towel. He was, she felt certain, gone. Gone. Whenever he was in a room or a house with her, she could feel his presence. She still felt cold in spite of the shower and the warmth of the room.

Had he gone for good?

The note was propped up on the little desk, near her Bible.

"We'll find a quiet place for lunch. Please. Sorry I yelled at you, babe. *J.*"

She dressed, putting on the spring suit and comfortable blouse she'd brought for traveling. Of course she would see him. She had promised she'd never run away from him again and she meant to keep that promise as best she could. She wasn't running out on him, she was walking. They needed time apart, space. She had decisions to make about him. Apparently, he had already made his decision. He wanted her, wanted her badly enough to offer to marry her. But he wanted his music, and if by some chance she didn't always please him, he'd very likely show that in his music.

His music was his message to the world. And right now, if Morning made him happy, his songs were meant to make the people who heard them feel good too. But if she displeased him—

It shouldn't, she knew, be like that. That part of them, their relationship, was all wrong!

She was brushing her still-damp hair when the knock came. She was certain it was Joe. She opened the door, and immediately all her self-promises and resolve to be cautious and distant left her.

"I'm sorry," he said quietly. "Can I please come in?"

She stepped back and he closed the door behind him.

"I just don't want you to go," he told her. "And if I act like a spoiled kid who got his candy taken away, that's my own stupid fault."

"We should have a talk about it," Morning said. "I shouldn't have just—Joe—wait—I really think we—" But she gave herself to his kiss, to the kisses that followed—on her lips, eyes, cheeks, throat. "Joe," she said after a moment, again wondering if he ever heard that pounding heart of hers, "I think we'd better go to lunch, so we don't—miss the plane."

"Yeah. Okay." He looked at her with those burning blue eyes. "When do we get married, Morning?"

"That's part of what we—"

"Why talk about it, why not just do it?"

"Joe, we've got to work out our differences first!" She gathered up her raincoat and the big umbrella.

"You don't need that," he told her, helping her with the raincoat. "My people will have an umbrella when we go out to the car."

She turned to look at him. "Oh? And will 'your people,' your well-paid slaves, be standing around outside the restaurant while we have lunch, just to make sure nobody bothers you? Or will they get to come inside with us and sit at another table, waiting for you to give the signal that we're ready to leave?"

"Hey," he said, "wait a minute—it isn't like that! Honey, those guys who work for me—we're buddies!"

"No," she heard herself saying relentlessly, "no, you

aren't buddies. Didn't it ever cross your mind that some of them—especially one of them—would do anything, no matter how vulgar, how filthy, how wrong, in order to keep you bringing in all that money?"

He frowned. "I never think about that. Look, I've got guys around me who take care of things that I really don't want to bother about! All I want to do is write my songs and play them and help people who need help whenever I can. To do that I need money. So I play my songs onstage."

"Joe, you told me yourself you hate getting up on a stage! You told me yourself you'd like to live on some boat you own so nobody could find you!"

"Listen, tell me what it is that makes you so hard to deal with, will you? Maybe," he said darkly, "I've got myself the kind of woman who can't let herself be happy—is that what I've got?"

She realized they were fighting—again. She said nothing, turning quickly away from him. Hot, quick tears stung her eyes.

"I'm sorry," she told him, "that I don't seem to be able to make you happy."

"I didn't say that."

She shook her head. "I honestly think we both ought to be able to see that it isn't working for us."

He had come up behind her, putting his warm hands on her shoulders.

"We've got to stop tearing each other up," he said, turning her around. "Honey, I never mean to make you cry. We'll come up with another plan for lunch."

He kissed her face, holding her, murmuring to her as if she were a frightened child.

But they would, she knew, quarrel again. And again, and again.

Morning followed him down the winding back staircase, past doors marked as fire exits, down until they came to a hallway on the main floor. Here were the hotel's huge kitchens. She could smell delicious food cooking. Nobody saw them as they walked down the hallway to the wide door beyond. The door looked like one that would lead to the outside, probably an alley. Joe had promised her that there would be no bodyguard, nobody else but the two of them, when they had lunch. They would, he'd said, find their own place, walking around Chicago until they spotted a private, quiet restaurant. Here, he wasn't as likely to be noticed, he told her, as he was in California or Nashville. So she was not to worry about anything. He would handle everything.

He looked behind them and pushed open the door.

The first thing that Morning saw was the rain, slamming down like a grey sheet. Then—from somewhere around the corner where they had been lingering, or maybe hiding, or maybe watching another door— came the females.

They made a crazed, attacking military onslaught, pushing, yelling, reaching out for Joe. He stood frozen for a few seconds, his arm around Morning. Then he pulled her along with him as he did what he seemed to think was the only escape: he ran.

He was very fast, very fast indeed. But Morning, slightly behind him, still hanging onto his hand, was fast too, used to running, even in the rain.

So apparently were many of his fans.

She sprinted along just behind Joe for perhaps two and a half city blocks, dodging traffic with him, darting out in front of cars that seemed too close for comfort. Finally, with the women on the other side of a truck that had stopped for a red light, she pulled her hand from his grasp and, breathing hard, heard her own ragged voice.

"This is crazy! I'm not going to do this!"

"Honey, there's the car—the limo. Come on, just across the street—"

"You go get in your fancy limousine! I'm going home!"

"Hey, don't—"

But the women were upon him, like a swarm of excited bees. As Morning ran on across the street alone, she saw Bobby, Joe's driver and bodyguard, jump out of the big car. Hadn't Joe said the car wouldn't be anywhere around, that they'd be completely alone?

She hurried by. She had lost the fine umbrella somewhere along the way.

Toby was sitting in the back seat of the car.

He had said he'd get rid of her.

She had just missed a flight from O'Hare. She phoned the hotel, asking that her luggage please be sent to the home of her parents. They were polite and eager to comply. People who could afford to stay in the penthouse were accorded every favor and respect, especially if Joe Hunter was paying the bill.

She went into one of the terminal's restrooms and tried to dry herself off by using the automatic hand-drier. Then she went to the coffee shop where there was no place to sit and eat or drink. Passengers stood at high tables and gobbled hot dogs and gulped coffee. She felt miserable.

It hadn't, of course, been Joe's fault. He had not known they would be there, that Toby had sworn he'd "see to things" and then true to his threat, had leaked word that Joe was leaving by a certain door and would be on the street in a few moments. In California, at that impromptu party at Joe's beach house, she had managed to hide her revulsion at the fans' reaction and even to be brightly light-hearted about it. But now she simply couldn't act that part. Not anymore.

She opened her purse to pay for the mug of coffee when she saw the little brown sack with the Bible in it, the one she'd bought that morning for Joe. She had meant to give it to him at lunch. Was there a post office anywhere in the airline's terminal? Even, she decided, if there were, she hadn't time, not if she wanted to get this next flight home.

Impulsively, she went into a phone booth and again dialed the magic number. To call the hotel and ask for Joe might have seemed more sensible, but she knew very well how hard his people made it for anybody to get through to him on a "regular" call.

The magic number was given only to people he wanted to talk to—anytime. The only other people she knew had it were his grandparents, who lived in a mansion outside of Nashville that he'd given them. If any other women had it…she wouldn't think about that now.

The same voice as before answered and asked her to remain in the phone booth. There was the usual series of clicks. Then, yet another voice asked her to please hold. More clicks—and finally, Joe's voice sounding gruff.

"This is Joe."

"This is…me," she said somewhat faintly. "Hello."

"Where are you? Are you okay?"

"At the airport and yes, I'm still rain-soaked but I'm fine."

There was a pause. "The airport," he said. "Look, will you wait there for me? I can be there in fifteen minutes, no more than twenty."

135

"Joe…please…no," she said softly. "Not this time."

Another pause. She realized her arms had begun to ache. Could that be because she was cold and wet, or was it some strange reaction to hearing his wounded voice—some yearning to hold him close, in her arms, shutting out the world.

"Not this time," he repeated. "When, then?"

"I don't know. I only know I want to go home. Please, let's try to leave each other and not…hurt. Not hurt ourselves or each other."

"Don't know how to do that," he said very nearly whispering. "Honey, just let me talk to you and explain to you—"

"Goodby," she said quickly. "Goodby." *My dearest*.

After hanging up on Joe, Morning phoned her mother from Chicago. It would be a comfort to be met by her mother, who would be very anxious indeed. Morning was not the sort of person given to unexpected visits or unannounced spur-of-the-moment droppings-in. Her job kept her in California most of the time, except for holidays and two weeks each summer.

Getting off the plane she saw her mother at once. For an instant, the nearly-forgotten shock of seeing her mother standing there without her dad jolted her. She mentally braced herself for the familiar sadness in her mother's brown eyes, hidden by a bright smile and a breezy way.

"Mom…hi." The two women hugged, then held each other at arm's length, as if to make appraisal.

"You've circles under your eyes, Morning," her mother said sternly. She was still a beautiful woman with silver brown hair and the same velvet eyes that Morning had. "Are you ill?"

"I'm fine. And, Mother, you look wonderful!" Her mother, she realized with a start, had none of that haunted look, that look she used to try so hard to hide—grief, misery, shock at what had happened to her husband. "Mother, is Daddy—"

She expected the answer: "About the same, dear. Doing as well as can be expected, I guess."

Their eyes met. Once, they would have asked, *What's that supposed to mean, 'as well as can be expected'? Maybe we ought to expect more!*

But now they were each determined, it seemed, to spare the other from any sorrow or pain they could.

Morning hugged her again. She was tired—she must be. She was close to crying, and that certainly wasn't like her. Never in public. Her father wouldn't have approved of that.

"You really do look wonderful," Morning said as they walked through the small airport together.

"I feel quite young, for your information," her mother said. "Do you have carryon luggage? Of course you do. You've nothing with you but your handbag."

"No," Morning said quickly, "I—the hotel is sending my things."

"The hotel? Where?"

"In Chicago, mother."

"What were you doing in Chicago?"

She touched her mother's gloved hand. "Let's wait until we're home."

"No luggage," her mother said darkly. "You must have been in quite a hurry to get away from there!"

In the car were sacks of groceries. Her mother explained she'd "rushed" to the grocery to get things Morning especially liked. She hoped nothing had spoiled. The weather had been lovely, just right. Oh, yes, her father enjoyed nice weather too, make no mistake about that.

Morning deliberately waited to ask questions, personal questions about the man her mother wanted to marry and how soon that would be. Could you, she wondered, divorce someone who had done nothing more than suddenly become very ill?

After a while, both women fell silent. It was nearly an hour's drive to her parents' house from the airport. The car radio was on but there was no need to worry about suddenly hearing one of Joe's songs because her mother only listened to classical. The two women were alike in many ways, but Morning had always felt more at ease with her dad.

"I hope you didn't eat that dreadful airplane food," her mother said suddenly. "Did you?"

Morning smiled. "Not even coffee."

"Because," her mother said, "I thought we might stop at that truck stop your dad used to like so much. We could have the breakfast special, if you like."

"Wonderful." She wondered, was her mother stalling, cleverly delaying their arrival at the house?

She remembered the restaurant part of the truck stop. It was big and noisy and clean and very ugly. There were a lot of men at tables who looked like husbands away from home. They were the truckers. They looked first at Morning, then at her mother as the women came in, but none of the men seemed rude or insulting. Those friends of Joe's, or some of the ones who professed to be his friends, had looked at her in a way that, if Joe knew, she was certain would enrage him, cause him to fire those people. Maybe she should have told him, been more open with him, talked to him more often about the Lord and—

She looked at her mother. Very slowly, right down to her fingertips, coldness was going over her, washing over her like cold, relentless rain.

"Do you want tea or coffee, Morning? Morning?"

"Oh. Ah…neither, thank you. Just the juice."

Her mother was watching her. "Do you mind telling me why you're angry with me? Have I said something to offend you? Perhaps I've been too nosy about why you were in Chicago."

"No," Morning said quickly. "I'm just a bit tired from the flight, that's all."

"It only took forty-five minutes, Morning." Her mother's voice was concerned. "It's because I told you I was thinking about getting married again."

"It's your life, Mother. Your decision."

"Yes. Now will you eat some nice eggs if I order them?"

"Of course," Morning said, smiling. But she was not hungry and the smile was not real. The cold feeling that might have been anger or outrage or just pain was still there inside her.

As they ate, her mother fussed over her, pouring coffee for her more as a matter of ritual than because Morning wanted it, urging her to put jam on the golden toast. They spoke very little. Morning tried to brace herself for the inevitable meeting with her mother's boyfriend. She realized she had come here not so much to see her mother as to spend some time with her dad. Even though he did not speak or seem to understand most of the time, he might, in some secret, vibrant, remembering part of himself, still suffer his great loss of family. Even now, he might know his wife wanted someone else.

If my father and mother cannot love each other in sickness and in health, for better or for worse, then

139

how can I expect Joe to go on loving me?

Even Christians betray each other sometimes. Marriage to a man like Joe Hunter could easily be a one-way ticket to hell—hell on earth at least.

Her mother was talking about how she had just finished having the house done. Her voice was excited, even happy, as she talked about the colors, cheerful colors, she said, warm colors, and a new rug in the dining room.

Yes, she probably would be getting married. It certainly sounded that way. Was there no such thing as human love, then? Was there no kind of love that never ended, that went on through all the grime and sorrow and mistakes of this world?

"...for your opinion on my ideas for the upstairs," her mother was saying brightly. "But I was in rather a hurry to get it done."

"I'm sure it's nice," Morning said automatically. "Very nice."

"Finished with your eggs?" her mother asked.

"Yes. I'm finished."

They drove on in that same strange silence. Morning mentally prepared herself for what she felt certain was to come. The new man in her mother's life would, at some time today or at the very latest tonight, present himself, and he and her mother would make the big announcement together. She would of course be expected to be very understanding about it, very adult, accepting it and even being happy for her mother's happiness.

Yes. She must try to feel that way. She wanted to, but she couldn't seem to.

They had now reached the outskirts of the University campus. Her mother turned onto a brick-paved side street where mostly faculty lived. She pulled up in front of "their" house—the one where Morning had grown up. It was a pleasant, two-story brick with green shutters and window boxes full of nodding flowers. Two cats, the same cats who'd hung around for the past eight years, crouched sleepily on the porch railing.

"I always wanted to live in this house," her mother said softly. They still sat in the car. Both looked at the house and its little rose garden in the side yard. During the first year after the stroke, her poor mother had lost heart and did not tend the roses, but still they flourished, unwatered except for the rain, never looked at, never cut and taken indoors for the window table or on the top shelf of her father's roll-top desk, where he sometimes feigned surprise at finding a bright, fat rose or a slender tea-sized pink one in a milk glass vase.

"I'm glad to see the roses looking so pretty," Morning said, knowing she must say something, that her mother was waiting for her to say how neat, how well-kept, everything looked. And her mother herself—the first, terrible, heart-broken year before Morning left to take the dream-job in San Francisco, she had to sometimes, some days, actually urge her mother to get dressed and to stop sitting by the window. Her mother had done much the same as her father was doing in the nursing home.

"It was the strangest thing about those roses," her mother said, her voice warm and a bit breathless, as if something wonderful was about to happen, some great secret revealed. "I used to glance at them that first year and think they would surely die, but they didn't. They're lovelier than ever, aren't they?"

"Yes, Mother."

"See that tree over there, the big oak? Well," her mother said, "when I was a student here, I used to sit right there and do my homework. I don't know who lived in this house then. And I used to tell myself that one day I'd fall in love and he would look like Gary Cooper and we would marry and live in this house, because it always seemed so beautiful to me."

"It still is." *You still are too.*

"And then when I met your father, the first thing I thought was that he didn't look a thing like what's-his-name—that actor, and that I loved your father's dear face and his way of always having a merry heart."

"Yes." Her throat was full of tears. *Don't*, she reminded herself, *please don't do that, don't cry, don't spoil her joy, for whatever reason it might be!*

"Morning," her mother said carefully. "I've something to tell you. And then we'll go in, and if you like, I'll cut some roses for the house, put one in your bedroom—"

"Tell me then."

The brown, level eyes, misted with what could only have been happiness, looked into Morning's own.

"I've brought him home," her mother said.

"You—you're actually living with—that man?"

"Oh no, of course not. I'm talking about your daddy. I've brought him home." In that moment, her mother looked like a schoolgirl in love. "That, you see, is why I did the house over."

"But on the telephone—that day on the phone, you said you were going to—"

"Yes, I did. I missed living with a man, frankly. Looking into a doorway and seeing a man there, smelling of shaving lotion, big feet propped on the lounge chair, that sort of thing. I didn't like a half-warmed bed, waking up and turning my face and seeing the other pillow was empty. It got very hard to take, living that way."

142

"He's better then? Daddy is—"

"Oh no, darling, I wouldn't want you to think that," her mother said at once. "It's just that *I'm* better, you see." She smiled into Morning's eyes. "All that time I was missing seeing a man in the house, it was not just *a* man, any man. It was your dad. And one night, I had a dream. I was walking through the house and I opened the door to his study and there he was, sitting there in his chair, just the way he used to do…"

Morning had taken her mother's hand and she held it tightly.

"…and he turned around and looked at me and he was himself again. Just the same. And I knew—I felt—that he might someday—"

"Oh Mother—Mother."

"So I went and got him and brought him home," her mother said. "And I told all the doctors they aren't God. They can't know for certain he'll never get better!"

Together, Morning and her mother gathered up the grocery sacks, carrying them into the house by way of the kitchen, just as they'd done when things were wonderful with her parents. The kitchen smelled of lemon wax and something garlicky bubbling from the black iron skillet. A neighbor, Mrs. Hobson, rose from the rocker by the window to hug Morning.

"I expect you'll be glad to see your dad again, Morning. I just took him a cup of tea. Perhaps you'd both like one."

"No thank you. Where's Dad? I'd like to just look in on him," Morning said, her voice shaking a bit. "In bed, or—"

"Not in bed, certainly not!" Mrs. Hobson's voice was firm. "In his study. Oh, Elizabeth, I put the sauce on for you, but I'm not sure it's just the way you do it.

Are you and Morning going to be able to make the lecture tomorrow evening, do you think?"

"I'm sure we will," her mother said. She looked at Morning. "Go on in, Morning. Go in and say hello to him."

"Yes." She felt very nervous. "Well, excuse me then. I'll help you put groceries away later, Mother."

The hallway rug was the same. Her mother had not changed that. It was maroon, with large white flowers, and here she used to stand, hiding behind the umbrella stand by the door, waiting for her dad to come home from teaching his classes. And when she saw him striding up the steps, young and handsome, looking for her because it was their own special, private game, she would nearly give herself away because she was so delighted.

He would come in the front door and in that magic moment, the game began in earnest.

"Where is she?" he would say loudly. "Where's my big doll? The one I bought at the toy store and put right there, behind that stand—"

And of course, Morning would convulse in giggles, giving her position away, and he would pick her up and throw her high in the air while she squealed, and then he would take her out to the kitchen and tell her mother that he had bought a very noisy doll for her and how did she like her surprise present?

Now, he sat by the window, not at his roll-top desk but in a rocking chair. There was a throw rug over his lap and his hands were folded. The hair on top of his head was getting thin; a little bald spot showed through. And he was thin, so much thinner, it seemed to her. The wide shoulders were still wide, but there seemed to be no flesh on them, under the new white shirt.

144

"Hello," she said, nearly whispering. "Hello, Daddy."

He didn't turn around. Morning went closer, until she stood in front of him. He had a little tray on his lap with a cup of tea and two cookies on a saucer beside the cup. His thin hands shook a little as he nibbled at one of the cookies. He did not look at her as she bent to lightly brush his cheek with a kiss.

Nothing had changed, he was no better. Yet everything had changed.

He was home. And his wife was still in love with him.

Chapter Nine

"I'd like for you both to move to San Francisco," Morning told her mother that first night. Her father was asleep in the double bed in the main bedroom, where his wife would join him later. Morning sat on the front porch with her mother in the creaky swing.

There were night sounds—crickets, a barking dog that made her think of Rags, a radio playing from an open upstairs window across the street at the house where rooms were rented to students.

"I'll take care of you both. You know I will. We could find a house, maybe out by Berkeley—"

"Wouldn't dream of it," her mother said sitting beside her on the swing. "I must remember to put some oil on this."

Her parents had said that years ago, but it never got oiled. Once, Morning had sat between them in the summers, listening dreamily to their grown-up conversation, hearing the steady, sleep-bringing creak of the swing chains.

"Mother! I want to! I feel responsible for you both. And it's only right—"

"It's only right that you live your own life, dear, and let me live mine. It's very good to know you're there for Dad and me, but we really don't want to move from here. I don't, and I feel sure Frank doesn't."

"In that case, if you really don't need me around, then I suppose it's okay for me to quit my job."

The swing stopped. "What? But I thought you said it's a perfectly wonderful—"

"It pays a lot of money, Mother. And I meet a lot of famous, rich people."

"Go on."

"That's it, essentially. I don't really enrich anybody's life, unless you want to say that having your game-room done in an African motif is an experience destined to change a life."

"I don't think it would change mine," her mother said. "Well, after you've quit your job, then what? I don't suppose you really want to come back here. You could, of course. You could take some classes. Or I could use my influence to get you a job typing for a professor. And maybe one fine day, you would marry somebody who teaches Romance languages. It doesn't sound too bad, does it?"

"I...don't think so, thanks."

"Which means you've already found someone you love, and nobody else will do."

"Something like that," Morning said. "But it...we...we both know we aren't really suited, and that we hurt one another, and maybe because I'm not as...as impulsive as Joe is, I'm always the one to walk away and be decent about it."

"And what does Joe do when you walk away?"

Morning smiled, remembering. "Looks for me. Finds me, makes me love him even more."

"I see. Well," her mother said cheerfully, "there's nothing like a persistent lover, is there? Your father used to wait for me right over there. I lived just three

148

blocks from here the summer we met, and I'd come here to study under the tree. He'd show up every day, right on time. Sometimes, when I didn't want to love him, when I just wanted to go on and be a lawyer, I wouldn't speak to him, and the next day he'd be there waiting, with flowers." She laughed. "Well, I think if this nice Christian man named Joe looks for you and finds you and makes you look as pretty as you do when you talk about him, you ought to call him up and invite him to come and meet us. You seem to be awfully lonely thinking about him."

"Mother...it isn't like that."

"Isn't like what, dear?"

"Joe can't...he can't just come here and ask for my hand, or something. He's—his last name is Hunter," she said, her voice low. "Joe Hunter, Mother."

"Who?"

Morning very nearly laughed. It had begun to seem to her that there wasn't a woman left in the world who didn't adore Joe Hunter.

"He's a country-rock star, Mother. Surely, you must have heard—"

"Oh yes, of course. *That* Joe Hunter!" She seemed to be considering this carefully. "I don't think your father would have minded," she said. "After all, he's a Christian."

"Mother...he isn't. He isn't, and that's the trouble with us."

"So, you're perfect and he isn't. Is that what you mean?"

Once again, the swing stopped as Morning sat up straighter.

"I didn't mean that at all! It's just that he seems to think I want him to wear a suit and tie and become some sort of paragon—"

149

"Didn't I read that he's always doing nice things for people? Wasn't there a little child he had flown to St. Jude's Hospital in Memphis, and he bought her parents a house so they could live there and be near her? And didn't I read—"

"Yes," Morning said. "But his music—"

"—his grandparents, don't they live in a home he bought for them down South?"

"Yes, Mother. In Nashville. And Joe probably gives money to people he never even heard of. I'm sure he doesn't really care about his money all that much and I'm sure he'd gladly give away all he has to help people if he thought that would solve problems for everybody. He's a very kind, generous man, yes."

"But he's not a Christian, you say?"

"No. He's not, I'm afraid."

"But does he believe that Jesus is the Christ, the Son of almighty God?"

"Mother, I don't know that! I mean, I've never...we've never talked about what his true beliefs are—"

"Then maybe you should," her mother said, very gently. "Before you judge him, as you're doing, maybe you should ask."

That night, Morning slept in the room that had been hers when she lived at home. It was small, with a slanted ceiling, a little window that looked out over the campus, and a windowseat, where teddy bears had once sat in solemn rows. Now, Morning sat there until late at night, thinking of Joe and her days with him.

The next morning, she jogged early, finally stopping at a drugstore just off campus to buy the out-of-town papers. When she got home, her parents were both in the back garden, having breakfast.

Morning joined them, going through the motions of

pretending all was well with her father. She sipped coffee and nibbled on toast as her mother smiled, chattering away to both of them, holding onto her husband's hand now and again, seeing that he had his lap shawl.

"He smiled a little at breakfast," her mother said later, in the kitchen. "Before I brought him inside, I'm just sure he smiled. Didn't you notice it?"

"Yes," Morning said, asking to be forgiven this loving fib. "Yes, I did."

She had meant to show her mother the papers, show her the review of Joe Hunter's performance in Kansas City, where he'd gone to do a concert right after Chicago. He had canceled, but re-booked, the paper said. Nobody knew why the sudden switch in his decision to finish out his tour after all.

She knew. It was because she had walked out on him.

She turned again to the story in the paper.

In a sudden switching of his laid-back, intelligent-man-in-love numbers done in Chicago, he has again become The Hunter, out for some kind of kill—wild, sensual, with a kind of concentrated and contained violence that drove them out of their minds last night—

Because she'd left him. That was why.

She decided not to read any more reviews, not for the rest of his tour.

She spent the next few evenings walking with her father across the campus, holding his arm, not talking to him as her mother talked to him, but close all the same. He always wore the same sweater. It had been a birthday present from her when she was twelve, bought from carefully saved baby-sitting money, and he had told her he'd "wear it forever." It was the same color as his eyes. Now they walked along silently and slowly, for his left foot dragged a bit, and when they came home they would sit on the porch swing, still silent, still close.

On Thursday, she went to a tea with her mother, and on Friday she bought them a big stereo, because her mother loved classical music and kept saying stereos were a nuisance, which meant she'd love having one but couldn't really afford it.

On Saturday, for some reason, she felt terribly uneasy. Telling herself it must have to do with her job and what Renée was going to say when she contacted her, Morning decided to go ahead and get the dreaded phone call over with.

San Francisco was two hours behind central time. Renée would very likely still be in her office.

She was. She seemed about to jump through the phone when Morning admitted she had not yet tried to contact Marcella Stratton, that she hadn't the slightest idea whether or not Marcella was still in Mexico, or even if she still planned to get married.

"Did someone there pass away, Morning?"

"What? No, of course not. Why would you—"

"Because," Renée said icily, "that's the only reason I can think of that would take you so far away from California, just when the firm has two very important and expensive accounts riding on you."

"I'm sorry if I've let you down, Renée. Look …frankly, I'm not calling to apologize. I'm calling to tell you I think it might serve your purpose better if you let somebody else work on the Hunter beach place and Miss Stratton's house too."

"What were you doing with him in Chicago? The papers said—"

"I told you, Joe Hunter and I aren't…never mind. Just get someone else to deal with those assignments, please."

"I can't believe you'd do this," Renée said in a fake stunned voice. "And you call yourself a Christian!"

"Stop that, Renée. All right…I'll call Marcella, not because I'm going to try to talk her into going ahead with her decoration plans, but to see if she's decided to make changes in her life."

"What kind of changes?"

Morning smiled. "She has some friends who want to save her life, you might say."

"Look," Renée said sharply, "I'm just about to go to one of those vile cocktail parties where people circulate and ask questions about other people. I'm bound to be asked if you and Joe Hunter—"

"We're friends," Morning told her. "Goodby for now, Renée."

She hung up quickly. *Friends*. Well, that was true, wasn't it?

She dialed Marcella's unlisted number in Bel Air. She didn't really expect an answer, but suddenly there was Marcella Stratton herself, answering the phone.

"Miss Stratton?"

"Depends on who has my number," the famous voice told her. "Who is this?"

"This is Morning Edford. I hope you didn't think I'd run out on you."

"Morning! Run out on me? Not at all! I'm the one who ran…all the way to Mexico, where I gained ten pounds and decided not to marry that adorable man. I feel ever so much better!"

"I'm glad," Morning said. "I mean—I'm glad you're feeling good about your decision."

"Well, there's something else," Marcella told her.

"That is...I...I thought one ought to be someplace else, anyplace else besides where I was, at the Hilton Hotel in Acapulco. I mean," she said, in that same husky, breathless voice, "I thought one should be in...in church or someplace like that."

Morning's heart seemed to beat faster. "Miss Stratton—Marcella—"

"But I was sitting on the balcony, by myself, and I just...asked. Asked Him to let me belong to Him. And almost at once, I seemed to be looking at myself, into my own head, and I saw that all this time, the perfect love I've been trying to find every time I got married was there all along. Only I just didn't know where to look for it."

Slowly, Morning let her breath out. "Do you mind if I come there and we can walk on the beach or have lunch or—"

"Wonderful, come ahead. Oh, I still want that house done. I'm going to move in there myself. The guest cottage is really a very nice house. I'll be using the main house for various things. I'd like to have about a hundred children staying there—writing on the walls in crayon and learning to swim in the pool—is that crazy?"

Morning smiled. "I don't think so at all. See you in Los Angeles, in a few days, Miss Stratton. God bless."

She felt immeasurably better. So much so that when she and her parents had dinner, she couldn't seem to stop talking about Marcella Stratton's quest for God and her conversion and how happy she seemed.

When her father had been kissed good night and was sleeping, the two women sat in the back garden, where they could look down the sloping summer grass to the campus.

"Strange," her mother said, "that Joe hasn't tried to

154

phone you. I thought you told me he always looked for and found you."

"Maybe this time he's decided I'm not worth the trouble."

"Maybe."

And after a while, when Morning stood up and started to go inside to bed, where she could cry silently, open-eyed, staring at the ceiling as she'd done as a child, her mother suddenly called to her from the rose garden.

"Hadn't we better go to bed?" Morning asked. "I thought we were going to be up at the crack of dawn and jog together, if you can get a neighbor to stay with Daddy." She leaned over the fragrant roses.

"I've something to tell you," her mother said, and Morning realized she'd been holding this back, perhaps trying to decide if she should talk about it.

"Morning, you haven't bought the papers the last few days and I don't think you've read the local paper and I know you don't watch news on television—"

"Mother," Morning said, her throat suddenly gone dry, "what is it? Please—what is it?"

"Someone was hurt—a girl at one of his concerts. I think it was Atlanta, last night. She got pushed in front of a car."

Yes, of course. Hadn't she always known that out of all that wild adoration, that insane reaching and clutching, something terrible would come?

She read the evening paper, standing in the kitchen under the bright overhead light. The girl was young, only twelve. She had come up to Atlanta from Scottsville with her older sister to see Joe Hunter's concert. Somehow, in the big push of people as he entered the theatre in downtown Atlanta, she was pushed back-

155

wards into the street. Now she was in serious condition.

Morning stayed in the kitchen a long time. Nearly an hour past her mother's quiet good night, even past the dimming of the library lights on the campus. She went to her father's study, carrying a cup of herbal tea. As if to feel close to him, even though he'd gone to bed upstairs, she sat in his chair by the long window that looked out over the back garden.

He is suffering, she thought clearly. *Joe is suffering—he's so gentle, tender, in spite of his anger and the way he lets his feelings come through in his music.*

On the roll-top desk, beside the last set of notes her father had lectured from was a book of poems. Her mother had given it to him on the last Christmas before his stroke. Morning picked it up and smiled as she saw her father's bookmark at Dylan Thomas's work.

Something, a part of a poem of his, came to her mind. How had it gone? Something about—

And then she found it, a part of "Fern Hill": "...such morning songs...the children, green and golden, follow...."

She stood up. *I have to talk to him*, she thought suddenly. The magic number—

But what could she do? What could she say to him that she hadn't said before? She couldn't make him change his musical message to those young people. His world was very hard for him to give up.

But he is suffering now. He needs me.

No. She couldn't help him. Maybe nobody could now.

She left on Sunday afternoon, after having gone quietly to church with her mother. She came home, helped prepare Sunday dinner, as she'd been taught to

156

do as a child, then went upstairs to pack.

When it came time to leave, she went to her father in the garden and leaned down to kiss his forehead. It was cool and he was wearing his old birthday sweater.

"I love you, Daddy. Pray for Joe and me."

It seemed to her, as she turned to go, that he had raised his head and turned it slightly to the left to watch her. And although he sat in the cool, shadowed part of the garden and she couldn't clearly see his face, she thought he gave her a long, wise, loving look.

Sometime on the flight to San Francisco, she decided she would, after all, use the magic phone number. She had planned to wait until she got a taxi at the airport and went home to her little Telegraph Hill house to call, but she realized she could not. She loved him and he needed her, needed her love and loyalty and support. She knew him—knew the dear, decent part of him, the well-brought-up side that spoke to women with deep respect. She knew the tender, compassionate side that gave so much money away and jumped into the sea to save a little dog. Yes, this kind of man would be suffering greatly over the accident.

Again the now-familiar voice answering the number, the clicks, the silence, another series of clicks, and then Joe.

"Who is this?"

"It's Morning."

"Oh," he said. Then: "Honey."

"Joe...I'm so sorry. I read—"

"Will you come here to me?"

"I just got *here*. I'm in San Francisco. Joe, I only wanted you to know how sorry I am."

"Look," he told her quickly, "I'm still in Atlanta. The call always goes first to my grandparents' house in

157

Nashville. Then their houseman puts it through to me wherever I am. I always let my grandparents know just where I am. They've been kind of hanging around the phone, waiting for you to get in touch. You might say I've talked about you to them."

"I see." She was in a phone booth. She leaned against it, closing her eyes. "I sent you something." The Bible. She had mailed it from the post office on campus the day after she got home.

"Yeah—I got it, honey. That was nice of you." He seemed to suddenly become awkward, or maybe it was difficult for him to talk about Christianity. "Morning, where are you in San Francisco? Still at the airport?"

"Yes. Are you going to be okay, Joe?"

"Don't know. It doesn't matter about me," he said. "The little girl—I'm hanging in here close, waiting for word. The last call said she's stabilizing. Honey, sit there and wait for me. I can get the next flight out and we'll have maybe a few hours there at the airport. I need to see you, Morning. Will you stay there? We can maybe walk around or have coffee—anything, just so I can hold your hand for a few minutes. I've canceled everything until...until the little girl—"

"Darling," she said quickly, "come...come on here. I'll be waiting. I'll meet your plane. Hurry."

He made up three hours' time, so it was just ten-thirty when he walked into the terminal, looking haggard, wearing very dark sunglasses, scruffy-looking jeans and boots and a faded pullover sweater. He looked more like a street bum than a world-renowned celebrity, and nobody had recognized him thus far, apparently, because he came from the plane quite alone.

Silently, like loving friends, they went at once into each other's arms and embraced. Then they walked,

158

arms around each other, rather aimlessly through the concourse.

"You hungry?" he asked, looking down at her.

"No. Joe, I think we're testing your good fortune at not being recognized a little too much. We really ought to leave the airport. You said you don't have to be back in Atlanta until tomorrow."

"No, honey. I said I'm not leaving Atlanta until she's better. Until I know for sure she's okay. Just this little time out to be with you."

She suddenly stopped walking. A teenage girl was staring at Joe, and she seemed about to start screaming or maybe worse, maybe to run to him and pull at his clothes.

"Joe, let's go to my house. This just isn't any good. Somebody is sure to recognize you!"

They took a taxi. Joe was silent, sitting in the darkest corner of the cab. Morning asked to be let out at the foot of the hill, so if he had been recognized, nobody would know exactly where they'd gone. Unless, of course, someone checked and discovered that she lived just off Napier Lane.

It was a little like being chased by demons. Like a loss of one's precious freedom. She hated it and it occurred to her that Joe did too. Only he didn't seem to ever try to change it.

He carried her suitcase up the wooden steps, and she walked beside him. Finally, there on the darkened little cottage porch, she felt that they were alone, that they were safe, for the moment.

"Wait," he said from the darkness. "Wait a second, Morning, I—"

The key was in the latch. "Joe, what—"

"Can't wait," he said softly, pulling her close to him, his mouth going to her ear. His voice was a thick whisper. "Can't wait to hold you, honey. Ahhh—I want to feel you close to me, Morning!"

They kissed, and this time a totally new kind of feeling flowed between them. He was, she knew, weary and frightened and horribly worried about the young girl. This time, Joe needed to cling to her. She had to be the strong one.

Holding her close, drawing on her strength, he murmured, "I just need this little time with you and then I'm going back."

"I know you haven't eaten," she said. "Come on. If we stay out here someone will know who you are. Joe?"

He looked down at her. His eyes were tortured.

"Okay," he said, "but I can't stay very long."

He sat out on the screened porch while she made the batter for omelets. She had bought some sourdough bread, the kind San Franciscans love, and she sliced that too, and put a little white bowl of butter on the table. From time to time she glanced out to the porch where he sat with his back to her, long legs stretched out, feet with the pointed toes of his boots sticking up on the porch railing. Finally, she went quietly out to him.

"Do you want to talk about what happened?" she asked, pulling up a little stool so she would be sitting close to him. Now, if she wanted to, she could curl her arms around his legs and close her eyes and listen to his quiet voice, deep, threaded always with Southern intonations. It was a beautiful, rich, husky-sad voice, famous not because of its range, for he really didn't sing like someone well trained, but because it was Joe's voice.

And Joe was the one they wanted, they adored, they

160

longed for. When he sang, it was some deep, secret part of himself that they heard—some lovely, charismatic charm that touched them, some power to make them feel as he wanted them to, to believe what he wanted them to.

No, he did not want to talk about it. He told her that very briefly and privately, sitting there close to her, with Morning's face touching his rough sleeve.

"I wish—" he said suddenly, and she opened her eyes. "You want to know what I wish, Morning?" His eyes were a deep, dark blue, full of need. "I wish we were married. I wish you were my wife and I could make love to you."

"So do I. I want that too," she said, "but—not now. Not yet. Not until—"

He looked away from her, going over to the window, half-turned from her. His misery and worry over the young girl had come back to him. There was no escape, not even in love-making. They both knew that.

"I don't know what you want from me," he said quietly. "I know you want some kind of change from me. Maybe I'm scared of what you want, not sure I can handle it. In this business, you meet a lot of scud, you're bound to. They want me to sing certain numbers in a certain way and they tell me that's what the kids want. It's got nothing to do with the kinds of music I really like."

"You were angry that night you played in Atlanta," she said, forcing herself to say the words. "You were wild and angry, and those are the feelings you give the people who come to listen to you! Joe, don't you know the power you have over them?" She was trembling a bit. "I grew up watching the way lovers ought to be, Joe. I grew up knowing my mother respected my father. That's the way I want to feel about you."

"Okay. I promise no more hard rock, just country and gospel-rock. I'll talk to Toby and tell him—"

"Toby would do anything in this world to break us up, Joe. Toby isn't going to let you change anything, not if he can help it."

He glared down at her.

"I'm supposed to be some kind of...influence over them? I make them crazy with my music? I make them fall in front of cars and have to go to the hospital and maybe—" suddenly, his voice cracked and very nearly broke. Morning realized with a shock that he was very close to weeping.

"Joe—"

He was at the window, where the city lights were spread out below the hill. "Just—leave me alone for awhile, okay? Go and finish fixing the meal because I've gotta get back to Atlanta."

"No," she said clearly. "No, you're going to listen to me! Joe, because you have this...power...for good or evil, you've got to make some kind of conscious choice. You're either going to tell those kids how to live and think and let them see how you live and think, or you might as well just get up there and strum your guitar and vomit on them and get paid for it!"

He was silent for a few seconds. "So what do I do?"

"You change, Joe. You change yourself from some idol they worship into a man they can admire and respect." Her voice was very soft now. "A man of God, that's the kind of man I'm talking about."

He said nothing. Morning went back out to her kitchen to get the omelets going. But she was glad she had said what she did. Finally, he came into the kitchen.

162

"I'll do it. But it's going to...take time—"

Which meant maybe. "I'll get you something to eat," she told him, turning back toward the stove.

"Honey—wait." He shook his head as if to clear it. "This probably isn't the best time for us to be making big changes. Right now I've got that girl on my mind. It wasn't my fault—it couldn't have been my fault," he said, "and yet I feel so rotten about it. There must have been an over-sell on tickets—"

"Other than making love with you," she told him suddenly, her voice thick, because it seemed to her that he was very close to weeping, "the only other thing I would like would be for you and my father to have been friends. And I'm not sure that...that either of those things will ever be granted to us."

He said nothing. He stood at the window silently, hands jammed into his pockets, staring out over the view of the city. He was so unusually quiet that it occured to Morning that he might be praying. Just maybe.

She began to set the little table. And she was still glad she had said what she did to him.

"We didn't have a fight, did we?" he asked as he put on his jacket after they'd finished eating. "You yelled a lot, but do we consider that a fight or what?"

For answer, she went over and put her face against his chest. She felt his hand on her face, very tenderly.

"I just want us to stay friends and not hurt each other," she told him.

"Friends. That's all you want?"

"For now, yes."

He kissed her—a long, slow, deep kiss. Then, he was

gone. At the bottom of the hill the taxi was waiting to take him to the airport.

Marcella Stratton's voice was very bright and cheerful on the telephone the following morning.

"I'm at the Fairmont," she said. "I'd much rather talk to you here in San Francisco than L.A. I was awfully glad to leave that place."

Morning, who had been sleeping at this early hour, pushed hair back from her face, and picked up the bedside clock. Seven-fifteen.

"It won't take me long to get dressed and get a taxi," she said. "I'll bring all the plans for your house. You did tell me you want me to go ahead with it, didn't you?"

"Oh yes, definitely yes. It's just that I won't be having *him* there. So you don't have to worry about *his* library, *his* darkroom, *his* separate hot tub—all of that nonsense. I meant it when I said I'd like to have lots and lots and lots of children running around. Can you handle making it the sort of house children would like?"

Morning smiled. "I think I can do that, yes. Shall I ring your room when I get to the hotel?"

"No," Marcella told her. "I'll be in the coffee shop."

"Eight-thirty okay?"

"Fine. And Morning?"

"Yes, Miss Stratton?"

"I read about what happened in Atlanta. And I know Joe Hunter is someone important to you. I'm very sorry."

Morning closed her eyes. "You aren't...telling me the girl—"

"You haven't read the papers, then?"

164

From outside, the shadow of rain against windows, cold, ugly—

"Is she dead?"

"She's much better. They've taken her off the critical list. Her condition is now listed as good."

"Thank God," Morning said, breathing again. "Joe will be so glad—"

"Wait, Morning," Marcella said carefully, "I'm sorry to tell you this, but Joe Hunter smashed up a car last night on his way from the Atlanta airport to the hospital."

Chapter Ten

Morning's only response was the slow release of breath that held off the pain, gave her time to gather her inner resources. *Please, Father. Don't let him be hurt.*

"He's fine, dear, so don't fret, please," Marcella told her. "The papers say he walked away from it. Apparently he was driving too fast."

"Yes. Thanks for letting me know."

Moments later, she dialed the magic number. This time, it was an older woman who answered in a lovely, lilting voice. "Yes? Who is this, please?"

"My name is Morning Edford and I was given this number in order to talk to Joe. There was something in the papers—"

"Could I take a message? This is his grandmother."

"Oh yes, of course. Would you call him in Atlanta for me and tell him I called?"

"Well I can put you right through, honey. You just hold on—"

"Wait—"

But it was too late. There went the series of clicks, small silences, and then a buzz, buzz. Someone picked up the receiver and a woman's voice said hello. For a second, confused, Morning thought it was still the grandmother. Then she realized it was not. Grandmother had hung up. *Click.*

This new, not-Southern, husky female voice was asking who was calling.

A nurse?

"Morning Edford. Is Mr. Hunter all right?"

The female voice seemed to be talking to someone else. "She wants to know if Joe's okay."

And another voice, a man's. "Who is she?"

Somewhat rudely, the female voice asked, "Who is this?"

"It's a friend of Joe's. Morning Edford." She wanted very much to hang up, but she didn't, because of her concern for Joe. He'd walked away from the accident. Marcella Stratton had said he'd walked away—

"Well, he's resting just now," the girl said, and someone, the man, was saying something Morning couldn't hear. "We'll tell him you called."

"Thank you," Morning said, hanging up. She had the strange clear feeling that something was wrong.

She showered, washed her hair, and blow-dried it, trying to think, to concentrate as she got ready to meet Marcella.

Could Joe be hurt and his people were keeping it a secret?

By the time she was ready to hurry down, get in the taxi she'd called, and keep her appointment, she was trembling. It was possible that they would do that. That Toby would—

Toby. It had been his voice in the background. So he was there in Atlanta with Joe, and of course, he would be screening all calls. She stared out at the bleak, rainy day. And there would be this, too, to contend with if she should marry him. Being away from him, not be-

168

ing able to get through to him. What if she should suddenly need him? If she were his wife—

"Stop," she said suddenly, aloud.

"Ma'am?" The cabbie looked at her in the mirror. "Hey," he said, "don't I know you? Aren't you the lady who asked to be let out so she could walk? That was about three weeks ago, I think."

"And you told me when you're troubled you talk to God?"

"Hey," he said, "it's a blessing to see you again. How you doin'?"

Morning looked closer at him. Yes, she knew she could trust him.

"You read the morning newspapers, don't you?"

"Sure. Why?"

"There was a story about Joe Hunter and—would you happen to know if he's okay? I mean, if the story said he's okay, I guess he couldn't be hurt, could he?"

"Look," he said, pulling to the curb, "I'm a married guy and I love the Lord, but if you need a friend, I'll buy us some coffee and we can talk about it. You look like you're about to fall apart."

"I guess I must look that way," she said. "Did you read the story?"

He handed her the morning *Chronicle*. "Here, read for yourself. And I'll buy you a donut with that coffee."

It only took about five seconds for her to scan what the paper said about the incident. Apparently it didn't seem that important, since nobody was hurt.

Not Joe. *Not the girl with him.*

"Listen," she heard herself saying, "I'm afraid I can't accept that coffee and donut offer. I've got a breakfast appointment." She folded the paper carefully, handing it to him. Funny, just then she felt nothing. No outrage.

169

No terrible pain. No deep sense of having been be-trayed—

"You going to be okay?" he asked. Then he smiled at her, this good man, a brother God placed in her path, maybe to ease the pain that would surely be coming. A girl had been in the car with Joe. She had met his plane at the airport, the story said, and they were returning to his hotel. "She was identified as Sara Carter, a former Las Vegas dancer Hunter reportedly met while appearing there last year. Both Ms. Carter and Mr. Hunter were treated at the hospital and released."

"You've got a ways to walk," he said, "all the way to the Fairmont. Maybe you better let me drive you there."

Morning nodded, not trusting herself to speak. Pain was beginning to seep into her consciousness. She closed her eyes, huddled there on the seat.

How could you do this to us, Joe?

Marcella was there in the coffee shop, wearing a floppy lavender hat and wide sunglasses. She sat in a back booth and waved when Morning walked in.

"Sorry I'm late," Morning told her, sitting down, get-ting work sheets from her briefcase. "I brought along the specs, and some color samples. I can easily modify them for the change in concept—"

"I suppose," Marcella said, golden eyes watching her, "you saw the morning papers."

"Yes."

"And you're upset because he was with another woman."

"I'd rather not talk about it if you don't mind," Morning said quietly. But inside her, there was the pain, the enormous outrage. "What he—what Joe

Hunter does is none of my business." She bent over the color samples.

There was a silence. Somehow, Morning felt much as she used to when she sat with her mother, working out some problem. Only Joe was more of a problem than any she had ever dreamed would come to her. She had never considered herself a complicated woman, but now she seemed to have become one. Right and wrong seemed all mixed up. Maybe she shouldn't be hurt—or even surprised—by what had happened.

And yet, she was.

"I never thought of myself as a nosy old busybody," Marcella said, dimpling. "But after all, I suppose I'm old enough to butt in whether I'm wanted or not. And famous enough. So please," she said, putting her small hand with its famous rings over Morning's, "please let me butt in and help you if I can, my dear!"

"He's not hurt," Morning said. "Nobody was hurt, and that's what really matters."

"It matters about the woman, doesn't it? I take it that came as a surprise to you." The waiter was hovering and Marcella smiled his way. "Bring lots of coffee, please. And fruit. Just so it looks pretty. Oh—if there's a page for me, I'm not available."

"Yes, Miss Stratton."

"I'm not engaged to Joe or—or anything like that," Morning said finally, as Marcella poured coffee for them both. "He has a perfect right to see anybody he wants."

"You needn't try to make me think this hasn't taken the wind from your sails, my dear, because I can see that it has. I don't think you're up to discussing business today. I think you and I should do something every woman knows about, the proverbial cure for all

171

sorts of things—" She smiled. "Shopping. Oh, not for me, but for the house. I want nothing but paintings for children in it, works of art they'd like to look at. So why don't we go to some of the shops and see what we can find?"

They found a lot—prints, originals, pastels and oils, reproductions and hot-off-the-easel sketches—all of animals, children, colorful balloons or flowers. Marcella took her to a well-known but private restaurant in Chinatown for lunch, and finally, well past three, they said goodbye.

"I'm reluctantly going back to Los Angeles," Marcella told her from the cab they'd shared to Telegraph Hill. "I'm starting a film there next week. You'll stay on with our plans for my house, won't you?"

"Of course. I think everything is settled. It's just a matter of getting the workmen in." Morning leaned over to briefly kiss Marcella's cheek. "Thank you very much for today."

"It didn't really help, though, did it?"

Morning smiled, "Surprisingly, it did."

She waved briefly and began the trudge up the hill to her house. She meant what she'd said. Being with someone who had so recently and with such obvious joy come to Christ had been like a lovely, unplanned-for ray of light in a world that the story about Joe had suddenly made dark for her.

There was, after all, life after Joe Hunter!

Her phone was ringing. She put down her purse and briefcase and started for it but suddenly stopped. It could be Joe. In fact, it very likely would be Joe, calling to explain or apologize. He would only have to tell her it was a mistake, a lie, and she would want to believe him so very much that in no time at all, they would be right back where they'd been before. He'd

172

be going on the same road in the same way and she would be caught up in it with him.

Please, Joe, give up!

But it went on ringing. When it did stop, it began again in ten minutes. Morning finally decided to take it off the hook. But it made such an outrageously persistent noise after a while that she unplugged it from the wall jack. Barefooted and carrying a cup of tea, she made her way to the porch to work on the plans for Marcella's big and little houses.

But she found she couldn't do it. She could not simply turn off the phone and forget about him. Whatever that girl had meant to him, she wouldn't have been there if Morning had done what he wanted. If she'd only found it within herself to forget her convictions, take his hand, and lead him to her bedroom where she could love him and hold his tired head and whisper words that gave him solace and hope. Just her telling him how much she loved him would have given him the strength, she felt sure, to go on back to Atlanta and face whatever had to be faced. Then he never would have been with anyone else. But then she wouldn't have been true to herself either.

Morning put down her cup. She carried the silent telephone back into her living room, plugging it in. Then, she sat down to wait for his phone call.

Waiting, she fell asleep. The jangle of the ringing jerked her awake and for a few seconds she thought she was in her bedroom. She picked up the phone, nearly dropping it. She must have been exhausted to sleep that hard—

"Hello? Hello?"

"Don't hang up on me," Joe said.

"I wasn't about to. What time is it?"

"I think it's maybe two. Were you asleep, honey?"

Honey. As if nothing had happened.

"No—I—I've been working on some things here, a project for a client and I must have dropped off."

"You read about it, I guess," he said, his voice low.

"Yes. I read about it. I'm glad you're okay." But she didn't sound at all glad about anything.

Don't, she told herself, *don't let being jealous come into this!*

"I didn't know she was going to be there," he said. "Honey, I swear to you, I didn't know she was going to be there to meet me!"

"Joe—don't—"

"I still can't figure it out! Somebody sent her to meet me, and if it'd been one of the back-up girls or even a wife of one of the guys in the band, or a secretary from the office or somebody like that—"

"Joe, did you call me up to talk about that?"

"Of course I did," he said. "I'm just glad I didn't get killed, so that woman could sell a story to one of the rags about how we were secret lovers or something! I didn't even remember who she was."

"I think the story printed her name, Joe. And said she was—that you'd known her—" No good. She shouldn't be talking about it to him.

"Morning, you've got to let me explain all of that."

She said nothing. She could feel his frustration. Well, how did he expect her to react? He had silently begged her to make love, but she had not. He had not insisted, but she had surely known of his need to be held and comforted, the way only a woman in love can comfort her beloved. Was it all so surprising that he would turn to someone else, someone more willing?

"I'm taking some time off," he told her. "Now that I know Wilma Jean is okay, I don't have to stay here in

Atlanta. Did you hear about her? She's fine. There wasn't anything broken. She'd just gone into shock. Now she's going to get to go home from the hospital."

"Yes. I'm very glad of that, Joe." The newspaper had said he'd been on his way, with his passenger in the car, to the hospital to check on the condition of twelve-year-old Wilma Jean Boother, who had been accidentally pushed into the path of a car at his concert on Saturday.

"How's the—the woman who was with you? How's Sara?"

Another silence. "The hospital released her. We were both lucky."

"I think," Morning said carefully, "I'd better say goodby now. It's very late and…and it all turned out okay. The little girl made it just fine and…and you're okay and so is—"

"Will you come to Nashville and stay with me, Morning? We can talk better there. My grandparents will be there. Honey, I've never taken another girl there, never. I want them to meet you. Will you come?"

Tears brimmed in her eyes. "Joe, every time something happens, it's like—like you're some kind of an addict! You run to hide in your music—or with a woman—instead of trying to get things worked out between us! Don't you understand that we haven't got even the most remote chance together if you're going to—"

"I told you," he said quietly, "I didn't ask for her to be there. Somebody sent her there to meet me. Because of the accident, the question never came up about her staying with me. I gave her a ride to the hotel because she said she was staying there. But I didn't know anything about how she got to the airport or

175

why she was there. I was too worried about Wilma Jean to suspect anything."

Toby, Morning thought. *Toby—again!* Sending a beautiful woman to get Joe's mind off his relationship with her, not knowing that there would be an accident. What a stroke of luck he must have thought that was, with the newspapers getting the story!

"Do you believe me, Morning?"

"Yes," she said quietly. "I believe you."

And she did. But it was just too much, all the problems. The women who clung to him, worshiped him, wanted him. Most of all his own not understanding how he could change all of that.

It was just too much.

"Then you'll come to Nashville? I need you, honey."

"No, Joe. No."

"Please. I'm leaving Atlanta today and I'll be in Nashville in a few hours. I want you to stay at my grandparents' place, meet my family—"

"It's no good," she said, her voice trembling dangerously. "Joe, I'm just not strong enough to take what life with you means!"

There was a long, cold silence. "Now you listen," he said finally. "Since I found you in my house in Carmel, I've never let you leave me for very long. We both know that. I've always come to find you again, because I love you. But not this time, Morning. This time, if you want me—if you want *us*—you've got to come look for me!"

He hung up the phone.

Chapter Eleven

This morning she would call Renée. If she could just stop thinking about Joe.

Usually, Joe would phone after an argument, call her up and tell her in a teasing way that he was sorry and she would be sorry too and for a while, it was wonderful being reunited. But it never lasted, not for very long.

His music would probably get wild again, crazy with anger again, the way it always did when they broke up. Or when she left. This time, she wouldn't hear about it. This time she wouldn't let herself read the papers. She would just concentrate on trying to get on with her life, without Joe at the center of it.

But no matter what they had said to each other, the fact that they loved one another would never change. She felt that in spite of everything, each had touched that deepest, sweetest part of the other's spirit, so that she had been able to believe they were surely blessed.

She had even thought she could change things about him. Convince him that he needed God to take over his life—and then marry him. But she had not been able to do any of those things.

Better this way, she kept thinking. *It's better this way.*

She decided to talk to Renée in person instead of calling her. She took a taxi and walked right through the outer office where the typists were, down the carpeted hallway to Renée's door, which was closed like a clenched fist.

Morning knocked, waited, knocked again, and went right on in. As usual, Renée was on the phone.

"Be with you in a moment, I've got two new assignments for you. One in Beverly Hills and one in the Valley."

Very casually, Morning leaned over Renée's glass-topped desk as Renée went on talking into the telephone, her voice smooth as oil. There was a notepad there, tiny sheets of sculptured paper with a feminine bouquet in one corner. Everything in this office was carefully calculated to give a certain air. Clients were supposed to feel that in this room dwelt a gracious woman who could send out little elves to change the paint and wallpaper and make their lives happy.

Morning wrote in a large, rather flowery script:

I QUIT.

Renée reached across the desk, picked up the paper, and adjusted her glasses. She was feeling very happy and she showed it. In Morning, she had found the perfect employee—faithful, very clever, charming to customers. And she didn't demand a big salary.

Suddenly, Renée stood up, nearly dropping the phone. She looked a bit pale under the peach-pink blusher.

"Look, darling," she said smoothly into the telephone, "I'll call you later, dearest. One of my top decorators just walked in. I think the lovely child probably wants more money."

178

She hung up and leaned back in her chair to gaze at Morning, who seemed about ready to leave.

"Would you mind telling me what this is all about?"

"I just did. I quit. I don't want to work for you anymore. I'm tired of working for somebody like you."

The carefully arched brows went upwards. "Oh? And has some other firm offered you a fatter salary? Is that what it really is?"

"No. I'm not going to work for somebody else. I just—Look," Morning said, "I'll finish up the assignments I've begun. That's Marcella's houses and Joe Hunter's house. There really isn't very much left for me to do there now. But I'm not taking any more work, Renée, and I mean that."

"You'll change your mind."

"No. I won't." Her voice was firm, and without another word to Renée, she left the office. She didn't, at this point, know exactly what she was going to make of her life without Joe in it, but whatever it was, it had to be better than working at a job that centered on the swift, sure acquisition of money.

She walked for nearly two hours after she left Renée's. The city—probably any city—seemed to take on a different feeling when Joe wasn't around. He would be in Nashville by this time. He would be having a rehearsal at the Opry House, that beautiful building he'd told her about. Nashville was his town now, his favorite place. And the fans would go crazy for him.

She stopped at the grocery and bought enough food to last a week. She would take time—time to read her Bible thoughtfully every morning, time to stop asking and start listening to God. She would go into her weedy little garden and get on her knees and make it pretty, as pretty as her mother's garden was. And as she worked she would listen. She would try to be still

179

and know that He is God, just as He'd told her to do.

The phone was ringing as she unlocked the door of her little rented house. At first she thought it would be Joe, because their pattern had been that she would leave him and he would find her.

But this time she suddenly knew it was not Joe, that he was not a man who would come back when he had told her he would not. There was a strength to him that she had seen only in flashes. Being away from her would hurt him, wound him, maybe tear him apart, just as it easily could do to her, but he would not come back to her again.

She put down the groceries and hurried to the telephone. If it was Renée—

"Hello," Morning said, somewhat cautiously. "Yes?"

"Morning, this is Mother."

"Oh, hi! Wait until I turn on the kettle—"

"No," her mother said. "You have to listen to me."

"I can listen better," Morning said, "with a cup of tea." When her mother did not say anything back, she suddenly put down the sack of groceries she'd been still holding. "Mother?"

"Yes. Yes—I'm here."

"What is it?"

There was a silence. And then her mother said the words that must have been an agony for her to say:

"Your daddy has gone to be with the Lord."

Morning let her breath out in a kind of sigh. When had she acquired this trick? At what moment in her life did she find that she could hold off pain for a little while, the way she was doing now? She was holding back the floodgates.

"Mother, I'll come at once."

"No, don't do that. I need a little time. A day or so."

"But—I want to come! I want to be with you...to help arrange—"

"Morning, that's all done. Your dad and I knew exactly what arrangements we wanted, and of course, I've got those plots—"

Were they actually talking this way? Talking about her dad?

"I just—need a little time alone with him," her mother said, "before anyone else looks at him. I want to sit with him."

"Yes." She closed her eyes. She needed to be brave, strong, understanding. Later, she could miss him, grieve for him. "When do you want me there, Mother?"

"Day after tomorrow, I guess. We'll have a tea that evening for your father's University friends. And—the funeral will be the next day." Her mother's voice wavered. "Goodby for now, dear."

It had begun to rain outside, not an uncommon thing in the city of San Francisco. She would not be able to go outside and kneel down and work in her garden today. She could, of course, make the plane reservation, but she had tonight and tomorrow and tomorrow night to get through before she could go home. *Shouldn't I be with Mother now?*

No. They've always been special. They've always been lovers in love. Let her have one more day to sit with him.

She went out back on the screened-in porch and sat down, with her legs curled under her and her arms folded across herself, huddled into a big sweater that had been her dad's before she gave him the new birthday sweater. This one was brown, with two small identical holes, one in each elbow. She had never mended them because it never seemed important.

And sometime that night, as she sat staring out at the rain-washed city beyond, she closed her eyes, bowed her head, and prayed, still not yielding to tears. An answer came:

God would not take my dad away completely until He replaced him in this world with goodness. Somewhere in my life, I'll find goodness repeating itself—

She needed to go to Joe. This time, she would be the one to go to him. She had to. Maybe it wasn't the right answer, but she had to go to him.

Impossible. Right now he was still in Nashville, and even though it was dawn now, tonight he would be doing a concert. Toby wouldn't let her see Joe. He'd do everything in his power not to let her get to him.

Halfway through trying to get a flight to Nashville she realized that because of the heavy fog it might not be possible. If she couldn't fly out from here, she'd have to drive as far as Denver, or someplace along the way, then catch a plane in order to be home in time. She would have to forget about seeing Joe, even for a few moments—

When the fog noticeably lifted, Morning was in her kitchen making coffee. She knew she was running away from her grief, yet she felt that if she could only have Joe hold her for a moment, just holding her so she could rest in his arms for a little while—then she knew she could get through this.

She called the airlines again, learned there would indeed be a flight leaving for points South, but she would have to hurry to make it and she'd have to go standby.

In the taxi, on the way to the airport, she tried to pray. But there didn't seem to be words inside her head just then. There were only need and the pain of losing a loved one. *Never mind*, she told herself, putting her weary head back on the seat of the taxi, *never mind. God knows what my need is, what my grief is. He knows.*

She looked at the back of the driver's head. No, it wasn't the same fellow—the Christian who had been so unexpectedly kind. In this moment, she felt terribly alone. She needed the comfort and understanding of God's people.

And she needed Joe.

Three standby people got seats and Morning was one of them. Tucked in her window seat, she wondered if she looked any different, if her manner or something else would give away what she was feeling. *Hurry,* she thought, *get me to Joe. Let me be in his arms for just a moment—please, Lord!*

In the airport at Nashville, in her confusion and fatigue, she took a wrong turn and ended up taking an extra fifteen minutes to find the right doors that would take her outside into the already dark evening, and to a taxi.

Somewhere along the way, sitting on the plane, she had decided not to call him. This way, she might have to face Toby, trying to get in to see Joe, but at least he couldn't hang up on her.

People were still surging to the Opry House and milling about inside. Most of them were probably under thirty, although not all of them. And not all of them or even most of them were women. Whole families were sharing soft drinks and popcorn in the brightly lighted foyer.

Morning went to the ticket office and asked if somebody could please call backstage. She gave Toby's name because she felt certain she would have to go through him.

"Please," she told the girl at the counter, "it's urgent."

"Look," the girl told her, counting out change, "if I called backstage everytime somebody wanted to get close to Joe Hunter—"

"Just tell Toby that Morning Edford is out here and that I have an urgent message for Joe."

The girl raised her eyes to look at Morning. Clearly, she wasn't certain whether or not she ought to believe this small, tired-looking, casually dressed young woman who was making such an outrageous request.

Was it, Morning was later to wonder, her own tired and somewhat rumpled appearance that caused the girl's eyes to soften suddenly and become understanding? Was it perhaps the desperation, the shock of obvious grief that led to a change of mind?

No. It was, she knew, God's hand that surely reached out and made the moment happen.

"Okay. Just go back and tell them what you told me. Once you get past here, you're okay. Besides," she said, "you don't have to deal with Toby."

"But—who will I—"

"I've got a little spy who keeps me informed about what's happening on stage. They're going to start late because Joe wanted to change the equipment."

"What?"

"He isn't doing it with strobes. So they have to change the lighting. Most of it they did this afternoon, but my spy told me that Joe said he's going to do a concert that's different. Anyway, it sounds wonderful—"

"Yes. Thanks for helping me."

He was going to do a concert that was different, he'd said.

Different—how?

Twice, someone asked where she was going. But nobody tried to stop her. Apparently, they remembered her, knew she was, or at least had been, Joe's girl. She thought she might get backstage before he began the show, but having to explain took up precious seconds. By the time she was actually backstage, among the strange faces of Joe's Nashville people whom she hadn't seen before, Joe was doing the first number of the show.

He sat on one of those high, three-legged stools, with his guitar strap catching the single spotlight that was on him. He looked, in that moment, like a man alone, very much alone. There was a pause, a hush, before the applause began and then rose like thunder. They, his fans, had always loved that song, "Love Shadows." It was low-key, full of remembering a time gone by. The lyrics were filled with a lovely, haunting story of separated lovers.

He sat looking out at them. Then the light went out, and in the blackout, he came backstage.

At first he didn't see her. She stood in the background, watching one of his aides wipe his face with a hand towel, seeing one of his Nashville people talking earnestly to him about the changes he'd decided on for this performance.

Then he saw her. He was noticeably startled. He stood there for a few seconds as the young man at his side went on talking about the upcoming changes. Joe said nothing.

But she could see the relief, the absolute joy flooding him. She had come back to him.

"Later," he said, still watching her, as if she might bolt and run. "Tell me later, Dave. My girl is over there, waiting."

He came over to her. "Welcome home," he said, beginning to smile into her eyes. "I never thought

185

you'd—Morning—" he said suddenly, seeing the look in her eyes. "Honey—what's wrong?"

But she could not speak, could not say the words. It was as if saying it made it absolutely so.

"Morning, let's go to the dressing room—" He would have walked off the show. He had already started to shoulder his way through the backstage people, one arm protectively around her.

"Joe—no—don't do this. I'll wait. I have to catch a plane for home but not—"

"What is it?" Her pain had become his own.

And then she leaned slightly against him, still not giving way, still not letting go.

"My dad died today. Mother called to tell me. I— have to go home, of course, but she said it would be better if I—give her a little time with him, you see—"

His hand was strong against her back, pressing her close to himself.

"Let me go with you."

"Yes," she said. "Of course, I want you there. I— need you there."

She raised her face to look at him. In that moment, it was as if they were already married, already husband and wife. Their love had somehow deepened, become beautiful.

The crowd was calling for him to come back on and sing again to them.

"I've done some things," he told her. "I fired Toby. I—listen—when I lost you this time, I finally understood you'd been right, Morning, right about everything. I want to make the changes, but I'm not sure how to begin—"

She smiled through her tears. Yes, God had replaced the good that left the world when He took her dad— replaced it by allowing Joe to come to Him. He would

186

show Joe how to use his talent and his charisma for the purposes of His holy kingdom.

Morning didn't ever have to think of leaving again. Now, Joe was what she had prayed he would become: a man of God, through Christ. He was clearly new at his role and a bit baffled, but God would surely lead him.

"Go on out and finish the show," she told him. "I'll be fine. I'll wait here for you."

"You sure?"

"Yes. Go on, Joe."

The thunder increased when he got on-stage. As he raised his hands for silence, that familiar, awed hush came over the audience.

"I'd like to surprise you a little bit now," he told them, standing downstage, close to them. "I'd like everybody to please stand up and join hands and join me in a song. I want to sing this song to honor my lady's daddy, who passed away today. I want to sing this song for him—"

"*Amazing Grace.*"

At first, they seemed hesitant and embarrassed, joining hands, touching hands with strangers. But then some began to sing the sweet words of praise, and others came on in. Within moments, their voices rang out, following Joe's.

There was a different feeling about what was happening out there. Even the people backstage sensed it. Behind Morning, two male voices began to sing along, joined in by several others.

Morning's heart swelled. Now, Joe would sing them a new song, a new kind of music, God's.

Promise Romances™ are available at your local bookstore or may be ordered directly from the publisher by sending $2.25 plus 75¢ (postage and handling) to the publisher for each book ordered.

If you are interested in joining Promise Romance™ Home Subscription Service, please check the appropriate box on the order form. We will be glad to send you more information and a copy of *The Love Letter*, the Promise Romance™ newsletter.

Send to: Etta Wilson
P. O. Box 141000
Nelson Place at Elm Hill Pike
Nashville, TN 37214-1000

☐ Yes! Please send me the Promise Romance titles I have checked on the back of this page.

I have enclosed _____ to cover the cost of the books ($2.25 each) ordered and 75¢ for postage and handling. Send check or money order. Allow four weeks for delivery.

☐ Yes! I am interested in learning more about the Promise Romance™ Home Subscription Service. Please send me more information and a *free* copy of *The Love Letter*.

Name _____

Address _____

City _____ State _____ Zip _____

Tennessee, California, and New York residents, please add applicable sales tax.

OTHER PROMISE ROMANCES ™
YOU WILL ENJOY

$2.25 each

Dear Reader:

I am committed to bringing you the kind of romantic novels you want to read. Please fill out the brief questionnaire below so we will know what you like most in Promise Romances™.

Mail to: Etta Wilson
Thomas Nelson Publishers
P.O. Box 141000
Nashville, Tenn. 37214

1. Why did you buy this Promise Romance™?

☐ Author
☐ Back cover description
☐ Christian story
☐ Cover art

☐ Recommendation from others
☐ Title
☐ Other_____

2. What did you like best about this book?

☐ Heroine
☐ Hero
☐ Christian elements

☐ Setting
☐ Story line
☐ Secondary characters

3. Where did you buy this book?

☐ Christian bookstore
☐ Supermarket
☐ Drugstore

☐ General bookstore
☐ Home subscription
☐ Other (specify)_____

4. Are you interested in buying other Promise Romances™?

   ☐ Very interested   ☐ Somewhat interested
                   ☐ Not interested

5. Please indicate your age group.
   ☐ Under 18   ☐ 25-34
   ☐ 18-24   ☐ 35-49   ☐ Over 50

6. Comments or suggestions?

7. Would you like to receive a free copy of the Promise Romance™ newsletter? If so, please fill in your name and address.

Name _____

Address _____

City _____ State _____ Zip _____